Pup-Napped!

Hey friend!

We're so glad that you're here to help us solve our very first mystery! This detective thing is way harder than it looks in the movies, but with your help we know we can solve this case. Get ready for an exciting adventure filled with twists, turns, and yummy bacon dog treats!

Now let's crack this case!

Love,
The Sister Detectives

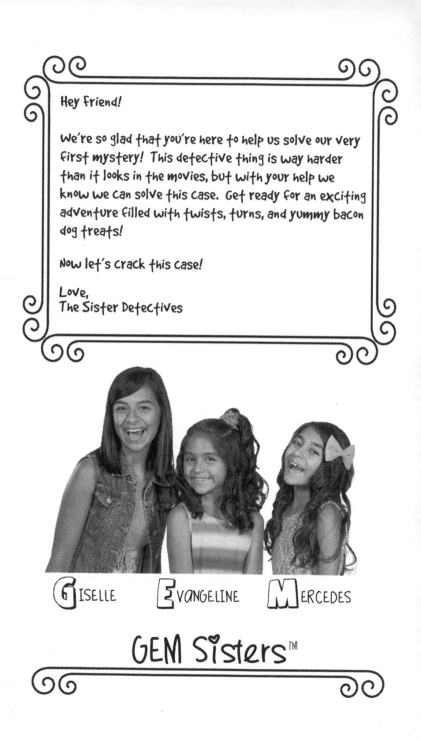

GISELLE   **E**VANGELINE   **M**ERCEDES

GEM Sisters™

Hang Out With GEM Sisters

Join the club!
www.gemsisters.club

Watch on YouTube
▶ /gemsisters

GEM MAIL

Write to us!
GEM Sisters
P.O. Box 3062
Glendale, CA 91221

Famous Fleas!

"Hey, I just got an idea," Mercedes said. "We find another gray and white husky, then we lie to the cute boy, and we tell him it's his dog. He gets a new best friend. I get my shoes. Case closed!"

"That's terrible. You can't just replace someone you love. What if I replaced you?" Giselle said to Mercedes.

Evangeline simply said, "Easy come easy go." She could feel another fight coming so she sat down and started watching videos of the missing dog Bingo on her phone.

"Two back flips in a row!" Evangeline gasped. "That's awesome sauce!"

"Stop! Pause the video. Scroll down to the comments," Giselle commanded.

Evangeline scrolled down slightly. There was a very mean comment from a user named "Hollywoof Dogs."

THIS DOG WAS TRAINED AT OUR CENTER AND WE WERE NEVER PAID. SEND US OUR MONEY OR YOU'LL BE SORRY.

Giselle's eyes grew wide in shock as she realized, "Bingo was PUP-NAPPED!"

Sister Detectives

Pup-Napped!

By MéLisa Lomelino
& Ryun Hovind

MéLisa and Ryun Productions
Los Angeles, CA

For our daughters Giselle, Evangeline, and Mercedes. The day you walked into our lives was the beginning of a grand adventure.

ISBN-13: 978-1-947775-00-8
ISBN-10: 1947775006
ISBN-13 eBook: 978-1-947775-01-5

First Printing: August 2017
MéLisa and Ryun Productions
P.O. Box 3062
Glendale, CA 91221

To see GEM Sisters™ videos visit: www.youtube.com/gemsisters
To see behind the scenes of the GEM Sisters™ check out their website: www.GEMSisters.club

Contents

CHAPTER 1

Dogs. There were dogs everywhere. Big ones,
little ones, short haired, long haired, and all
different colors. An adorable brown beagle
puppy played with his hamburger chew toy.
The toy squeaked over and over then instantly
stopped when the pug let out a loud smelly fart.
The dog owners started laughing as they held
their noses.

Evangeline couldn't help but giggle. "This is
gonna be fun. I can't wait to talk to the dogs,"
she said.

The youngest of three sisters, nine-year-
old Evangeline, was dressed in her usual
rainbow colored clothes to match her spunky
personality. Her dark brown eyes shined bright
against her beautiful brown skin as she smiled.
She was about to say hi to the dogs when her
tummy let out a loud growl. "I need a snack!"

"Shh!" Giselle insisted. "Mom and Dad put me in charge, so tell your stomach to be quiet."

Giselle was the oldest at fourteen. She was much taller than her sisters and had short dark brown hair. She didn't wear lots of makeup, but instead liked to wear tons of jewelry. She tried to keep her sisters out of trouble, but somehow trouble always seemed to find them.

"My new boots! They're ruined," Mercedes screamed at the top of her lungs. She pointed to the poop pile that she had just stepped in.

Mercedes, the middle sister at ten years old, looked glam every day and was always trying to be the center of attention. She enjoyed getting lots of compliments on her beautiful hazel eyes, light brown skin, and long brown hair. She loved fashion and usually wore her favorite color pink.

Mercedes quickly grabbed her pink sparkly phone and started filming. "Guys look at this tragedy!" she whined.

Giselle grabbed Mercedes' phone out of her hand. "Not now," she lectured.

"Our fans need to know everything that happens in our day, good or bad," argued Mercedes.

"Fine," groaned Giselle. "But go film outside.

And wipe off your boots while you're out there because you smell. Like really bad."

Giselle and Evangeline both held their noses and made gagging noises.

Mercedes turned to address the group of dogs. "I'm going to find out which one of you did this!" She grabbed her phone and stormed off.

Evangeline leaned over and whispered to the adorable brown pug, "Don't worry your secret is safe with me."

Giselle laughed out loud as she typed on her phone. Evangeline leaned over and saw a picture of Mercedes on the screen. She was making a grossed out face and Giselle had added a poop emoji along with a crown on Mercedes' head. The caption read "Dog Poop Princess."

"And post," said Giselle with a smile as the photo went up on their GEM Sisters' website.

GEM Sisters stood for the sisters' names Giselle, Evangeline, and Mercedes. Together they made funny online videos for their popular website. But today they were hanging out on a film set because their parents were casting a new dog treats commercial.

The girls' parents owned a small film production company in Los Angeles, California.

They were always looking for the next project, hoping it would push them into big Hollywood movies and TV shows. The owners and their dogs listened carefully.

Dad was holding a bacon dog treat high in the air and Mom was on her hands and knees acting like a dog. First, she walked in a circle, her long blonde hair hanging in her face. Then she squatted on her heels. Mom jumped up into the air, barking as she grabbed the dog treat in her mouth, then landed back on the ground.

"Can your dogs do that?" Mom asked the owners, as she spat out the dog treat and popped a mint into her mouth. "When it's your turn, show us that, plus any special tricks your dog can do."

"Mom!" shouted Mercedes from across the room. Mercedes' hair curls bounced as she stormed toward them.

"We'll start in five minutes," said Mom to the group as she rushed over to Mercedes.

"You're just in time. We're having auditions to pick the perfect dog for the commercial," smiled Mom. She could tell Mercedes was having a drama queen moment and hoped the word "audition" would stop her in her tracks.

"But Mom, Giselle posted this mean picture

of me. And it's not my good side," said Mercedes as she showed Mom the photo.

"Girls I know you're probably tired from school, but we really need you to get along while we're working," lectured Mom.

"No more posting funny pictures until we're done. Okay poop princess?" said Dad unable to hide a giggle.

Mercedes folded her arms and glared at Giselle. Then all three girls nodded yes.

Mom and Dad weren't like most parents. As filmmakers, they were usually distracted by their latest project. This meant that the girls often had to be independent when it came to homework, food, and chores. But the good thing about having filmmaking parents was that the sisters always had help making their funny videos.

"I'm going to go set up the camera," said Dad as he turned to leave and gave Mom a kiss on the cheek.

"Don't worry we'll get our homework done during the auditions," said Giselle. She pulled out a giant heavy book from her backpack. Giselle took school very seriously. She was over-prepared for every subject and always got straight A's. She looked to her sisters to follow her lead, but they ignored her.

Mercedes' only goal in life was to be famous so she saw every audition as a chance to make it big. "Mom! I had the most amazing idea! Wouldn't it be perfect if I was the star of the commercial? And this poodle could be my puppy. We'd be #adorbs," Mercedes said as she picked up the black poodle next to her. She quickly took a picture on her phone.

"Mercedes, the answer is still no. Fame can wait. Homework now!" Mom said as she left. Mom was crazy obsessed with her career, but when you least expected it, she would act like a normal mom. Homework was one of those times.

"Give it up Mercedes," Giselle said. "Quit bugging Mom. She's busy."

Mercedes set down the dog and went back to taking kissy face pictures. Giselle noticed Evangeline on her hands and knees staring silently at a group of dogs. Curiously, she sat down next to her.

"See that dog?" Evangeline asked Giselle.

"Uh, which dog? The whole room is full of dogs," Giselle said annoyed.

"The one that just stuck his tongue out at me," motioned Evangeline.

"What are you talking about?" Giselle asked shaking her head.

"The short tan one with the fluffy face. He's staring at me. See? He just stuck his tongue out again!"

"Don't be ridiculous. He's not sticking his tongue out at you. That's a terrier dog. That's what they look like," Giselle explained.

Evangeline had a quirky way of seeing things and could rarely be convinced she wasn't right. "Oh, it's on dog dude," Evangeline taunted. She leaned in, locked eyes with the terrier, and refused to look away.

"I can't believe you're having a staring contest with a dog," said Giselle. She didn't know why she was so surprised. Evangeline was always up to something strange.

Evangeline ignored her sister, putting all of her energy into her laser gaze. She and the dog's eyes locked. But after a moment, he turned away and started chewing on his foot.

"Ha! The victory is mine!" shouted Evangeline. "I wonder if any of these dogs have learned to speak human?" she said as she wandered off.

Mercedes continued to complain to Giselle. "How can I make Mom and Dad understand?

They NEED me in this commercial. None of these dogs look as cute as me," she said waving her hand from head to toe. "Look at my sad puppy dog face," Mercedes said, pouting her lips.

"You're right Mercedes. You do look like a dog," laughed Giselle. Giselle learned long ago when Mercedes has her heart set on something she will push and push until she gets her way. It's best not to get involved.

"Did I tell you about my essay?" asked Giselle as she flipped the pages in her notebook switching subjects. "I'm calling it *The Secrets of George Washington*. Did you know that he created a whole network of spies during the Revolutionary War? It's so cool. He had all of these secret agents who would collect information and use secret messages to-"

Click! Mercedes took a selfie as she let out a loud yawn. She read aloud as she typed a caption for her picture, "When you don't want to do your homework." Her phone beeped the sound of the photo posting online.

Giselle groaned. "You know school is important and someday-"

Mercedes quickly faked a phone call. "Ooh sorry. Hold that lecture. Gotta take this. Hello, nobody?" she said as she walked away.

Just then Evangeline crawled up to Giselle on all fours and licked her hand.

"Gross!" yelled Giselle. "Why did you do that?"

Evangeline looked at Giselle with a confused face. Then she licked Giselle's hand again.

"Stop it!" Giselle commanded. Giselle glared at Evangeline who smiled and said nothing. "Evangeline! Speak!"

"Arf Arf Arf!" chirped Evangeline.

"Speak English," Giselle said annoyed.

"You understood me. See that wasn't so hard," explained Evangeline. "So then why can't these dogs figure out how to speak human?"

Giselle decided not to respond. Instead, she chose to go back to writing. "Right now my essay is five pages long, so I have to edit it down. And I present it to my class next week."

Evangeline looked down and said, "Really? So soon?"

"I know. Right? I'm nervous I'm not going to get it done on time. It's so hard to choose what parts to cut. All of the spy stories are so interesting," Giselle said. She was happy that Evangeline was listening for once.

Evangeline replied but it wasn't to Giselle,

"Yeah, I totally agree." Giselle didn't notice.

"Really Evangeline? Do you want to know more about spies?" asked Giselle.

Evangeline looked at her confused.

"Huh? I wasn't talking to you. I was talking to my tummy. It's telling me it's time to eat again," she explained. "There's just no stopping it when it gets this way."

Giselle scowled and turned back to her book. She decided to give up on trying to make her sisters interested in her homework.

Evangeline wandered over to where Mom and Dad were auditioning the dogs. A flashy black poodle with pink bows and a pink skirt danced to the music. The owner danced along as the dog got up on her hind legs. "Shake your booty," the song said as the poodle wiggled her tail.

"Dog-tastic!" said Evangeline. Then she grabbed her tummy and rolled on the ground like she was in pain. "Mom snack... dying... can't hold on much longer..."

Dad stopped the music. "Impressive! We'll be in touch," he said to the poodle's owner.

"You can have a healthy snack," Mom said reaching into her purse. "Oh look, you guys never ate these from yesterday." She pulled out a plastic bag full of warm wilted baby carrots and celery sticks.

"How about these instead?" asked Evangeline as she grabbed a can of bacon treats from the set. "You know I love bacon!"

Mom took the can. "These treats are for dogs. You can have the bag of carrots."

Evangeline couldn't hide her grossed out face. "I remember why we didn't eat them," she muttered to herself as she smashed a warm carrot between her fingers.

"Now, don't eat too much or you won't be hungry for dinner," Mom said. "Next!" she yelled as she motioned for Evangeline to leave.

Evangeline tried to feed the healthy snacks to a nearby pug dog, but he didn't even bother to sniff them.

"I agree," said Evangeline as she dropped the bag of vegetables into the garbage.

The dog barked and barked as Evangeline listened.

"I understand exactly what you're saying. Ya know, you've got the mind talk down perfect. Now, I just have to teach you how to speak human out loud."

The dog turned his head and barked again. Evangeline followed the dog's gaze over to the snack table.

"That's a great idea!" she said to the pug.

They both snuck over to the snack table. She knew she wasn't supposed to be there, but this was the gold mine of snacks.

"I won't tell if you don't," she said to the pug with a wink.

Suddenly she spotted super yummy chocolate mini cupcakes with fluffy vanilla frosting. They whispered her name, begging her to eat them.

Wanting to impress her new dog friend, she tossed the cupcake high in the air and tried to catch it in her mouth.

Smack! It landed on the ground. Again she threw another cupcake into the air, not quite as high as before. And smack! Missed again. Over and over she tossed and missed until she realized there was only one cupcake left.

She grabbed it and considered just popping it into her mouth. "Nah. That would be cheating," she told the pug. She launched it up extra high in the air, opening her mouth really wide and closing her eyes for luck. Seconds passed. No smack. Nothing. Where did it go?

"ARGH! Who did this?" yelled Mercedes as she grabbed the cupcake on her head. She ran toward the snack table and pulled off the cupcake which left a huge glob of frosting in her hair.

Evangeline thought quickly and pointed to the pug next to her. His pink tongue sticking out made him look extra guilty.

Mercedes threw the cupcake down and glared at the dog. With her finger pointing toward him, she said, "It was you with the poop too, wasn't it! You will never, ever work in this town again! Got it?" Mercedes stormed off.

Evangeline looked at the confused dog. "Sorry dude. Thanks for taking the blame. She's still mad at me for last week when I used her jewelry box for my new worm farm."

"Arf," the dog barked.

"You're right. We can't waste these perfectly good cupcakes. And besides, most of them landed on the cupcake paper so there's not too much dirt."

The dog came closer and licked the frosting on her shoe.

Evangeline gathered up the cupcakes on the ground and began shoveling them in her mouth. "I'd give you one, but you can't have chocolate, on account of you being a dog and all."

The pug yelped to get Evangeline's attention. Her dad was coming toward them. She quickly shoved another cupcake in her mouth.

"Why was Mercedes yelling? Is she okay?" asked Dad.

Evangeline looked like a chipmunk, her cheeks stuffed with cupcake. She made an "I don't know" motion.

Dad shrugged it off too. "Well, she seems okay now, and I see Giselle is getting her homework done. You having fun?" Dad asked.

Evangeline nodded yes and continued to enjoy her cupcake.

"Looks like you found a friend," Dad said nodding toward the pug who was still licking Evangeline's shoes.

"Yup, he wants me to teach him how to speak human," she said.

Her dad chuckled. He always enjoyed Evangeline's quirky humor. "It's going to be *ruff* to find the right dog today. Get it? Ruff?" joked Dad. "Maybe instead of organic bacon treats we should do a commercial for pup-peroni pizza treats. Pup-peroni!" Dad said as he laughed. Dad loved to tell jokes and once he got started it was hard to get him to stop.

Evangeline let out a fake laugh, but suddenly was craving another cupcake. Those things were addictive. She looked down and saw that the pug had moved on from licking her shoes to licking the vanilla frosting from the cupcake Mercedes had thrown on the ground.

Nope. Even she drew the line at eating dog drool. Yuck! She spotted one under the table that she had missed earlier. She wondered if she could get it without her dad noticing.

Evangeline sat down and scratched the pug's head with one hand. She kept eye contact with her dad, pretending to listen. Her other hand searched under the table for the last cupcake. She reached further and finally her fingers felt the frosting. Just then she noticed her dad had stopped talking. He was looking at her expecting her to respond.

Evangeline quickly chuckled as she thought of something to say, "Hey Dad what do you call a dog's favorite dessert? Pupcakes!"

"Good one!" Dad laughed. "Hey! Where are all the cupcakes? I need some sugar to help me get through the rest of these auditions," exclaimed Dad. "We've been auditioning dogs since you girls left for school this morning."

Evangeline grabbed the cupcake that the

dog had been licking as her dad searched the snack table. The icing was pretty thin on top. She hoped her dad wouldn't notice.

"I won't tell Mom if you won't," said Evangeline, as she handed the dog drool cupcake to her dad.

"Mmmm good! Thanks sweetie. This will be our little secret," Dad said as he took a bite. Evangeline giggled as she popped the good cupcake in her mouth.

Dad's walkie talkie buzzed. It was as if Mom knew he was eating junk food again. Mom's walkie talkie voice said, "I'm done with Mercedes' hair drama. Somehow she got frosting in it."

Dad looked to Evangeline who shrugged her shoulders and smiled.

"Let's call up the next dog," Dad said into the walkie as he ran back to set.

The pug chased after Dad causing Evangeline to follow. Evangeline caught up to the dog in time and stopped him before he ran onto the set.

"It's not your turn," she said to the dog. "And if you really want to book this commercial, then you need to learn to speak human."

Just then a cute teen boy with brown hair, a

crooked smile, and gorgeous bangs over his blue eyes walked up to the video camera. He had a skateboard under one arm, but no dog.

"Hi I'm Austen," he said.

Mom looked at him confused, "Uh hi Austen. Glad you could make it, but in case you didn't know, we're auditioning dogs today."

"Yeah. That's why I'm here. My dog's name is Bingo. He's epic. Like perfect. He's totally the star you want for this commercial."

"Is he an invisible dog?" said Mom as she looked around the set.

Evangeline eagerly started looking. "No offense, but an invisible dog is even cooler than a human speaking dog," she said to the pug.

"My dog is an amazing white husky puppy," said Austen upset. He held up a flyer with a picture of Bingo. "I'm trying to tell you. My dog is missing!"

CHAPTER 2

Mom put a comforting hand on Austen's shoulder as he quickly wiped away his tears on his sleeve.

Evangeline watched the scene and leaned over to the pug to whisper, "Sorry about saying the invisible dog was cooler than you. I hope you will still let me teach you how to speak human."

"Arf!" barked the pug. Then he turned and ran back to his owner.

"Your loss," Evangeline called out. "Looks like the search for a human speaking dog continues," she said to herself.

"Austen, we're really sorry about your dog, but we're on a schedule here," explained Mom.

"Dude! Like, wait," Austen said holding up his phone. "This will blow your mind. You gotta see the awesome tricks I taught him. My puppy

Bingo is like animalistic."

"Animal what?" asked Dad.

"Like, no other dog is near as cool as Bingo. He's epic!" explained Austen. "Here! I can prove it. Check out these videos." Austen searched through the videos on his phone.

"I'm sorry. You seem like a really nice kid, but we can't audition a dog if he's not here," Mom said kindly.

"Yeah man sorry. Rules are rules," Dad chimed in.

Just then Mom noticed the cupcake crumbs on the corner of Dad's mouth. She brushed the crumbs off with her fingers. "And it's important to follow rules isn't it?" Mom said to Dad with a smirk.

"Next!" yelled Dad quickly changing the subject.

Austen put his head down and started walking off the set. As he passed Evangeline she stopped him. She had heard him say "dog tricks" and wanted to know more. Maybe he had trained his dog to speak human.

"Hey, can I see the video? My name is Evangeline. My parents are in charge here so if I like what I see maybe I can put in a good word for your dog."

Austen was desperate to get Bingo this commercial. "Get ready for amazing times a million," he said as he handed the phone to Evangeline.

On screen was a video starring a cute white husky puppy with sky blue eyes. "A husky! You've definitely got my attention," she said excitedly.

Evangeline's eyes grew wider with each trick. Bingo jumped through hoops, did yoga poses, rode a skateboard, and a surfboard. "Wow, he's definitely got it," she said with a smile.

Austen beamed, proud of Bingo. "Wait til you see the last trick. It's for sure something only my Bingo can do. Like, it's the move that'll make him a star!" said Austen.

On the video Bingo did one back flip and then instantly did another.

"Two back flips in a row!" Evangeline gasped. "That's awesome sauce! Bingo doesn't by any chance talk human, does he?"

"Uh, no," said Austen, puzzled by the question.

"Nevermind. He's still the best I've seen today. Come on. I gotta show this to my sisters."

Austen followed Evangeline to where Giselle

and Mercedes were sitting on the floor. They were both too busy to notice.

"Hey bookworm! Mirror face! You guys have to check out this dog. He's the coolest!" said Evangeline.

"More dogs? No thank you," said Mercedes annoyed as she continued to check her phone.

"I'm trying to finish my report," groaned Giselle. She looked up to lecture Evangeline, but her face instantly turned into a sheepish smile at the sight of Austen.

"Hey I'm Austen," he said as he extended his hand to Giselle.

Giselle grabbed Austen's hand and he pulled her to her feet. "Hi... gorgeous. I mean hi I'm Giselle," she said trying to hide her mistake.

Evangeline could tell some weird lovey dovey stuff was going on so she quickly changed the mood by pressing play on the video. Giselle was impressed. She laughed at the dog's tricks. "Wow, this dog is something else," she said out loud. But to herself, she thought, *and Austen is something else too. He's so dreamy and so talented to train a dog like that.*

The laughing got Mercedes' attention. She jumped up to see what everyone was watching.

"A double back flip! Wow!" Giselle laughed.

"That's crazy," she laughed louder and choked out a snort laugh. She put her hand to her mouth in horror. How awkward. She couldn't believe she had just done that.

"Wait a second," demanded Mercedes. "Is that for real?

"For sure. I don't do trick editing. My dog Bingo is one hundred percent amazing on his own. He's the only dog I've seen that can do two back flips."

"Not the flips, I mean the views. Does he for real have a million views on that video?"

"Yeah."

"A dog has more fans than me? My life is so unfair!" whined Mercedes.

"Bingo is missing," explained Evangeline, ignoring Mercedes' complaining.

Austen started to tear up again. "I just miss him so much. This was totally our chance to get Bingo to the next level," he said sniffing back his tears. "Yesterday we were practicing in the front yard playing frisbee. I ran into the house to get a hoop for him to jump through. When I came back, he was gone."

Giselle stared into Austen's deep blue eyes. Mercedes' eyes showed that she was still in shock that a dog was more famous than her.

Evangeline was the only one who seemed to care about the missing dog.

"None of it matters now. I like don't even care about TV or money or fame and stuff. I just want Bingo back. He's my best friend," said Austen sadly.

"We can help you find Bingo!" announced Evangeline. "He needs our help and he's the perfect dog for Mom and Dad's commercial."

Giselle and Mercedes couldn't hide their shocked faces. What was Evangeline thinking? But when Austen's face turned suddenly hopeful, Giselle gave in.

"Of course we can help find your dreamy puppy," said Giselle. "I mean you're so cute... I mean HE'S too cute not to help." Giselle decided to stop talking before she said something worse.

"Thank you!" said Austen as he hugged Giselle, who melted in his arms.

"Uh, count me out," said Mercedes. "Sorry about your dog Bongo or whatever, but I have a strict social media schedule to keep."

Austen let go of Giselle who didn't realize the hug was over. Thankfully Evangeline noticed and pulled her back before it got too awkward.

"I've got these flyers I made," explained Austen as he passed them out to the girls.

"$500 reward!" yelled Mercedes as she grabbed the flyer. "What are we waiting for? This dog is not going to find himself!"

Giselle glared at Mercedes who was obviously only interested in the money. "What have you done so far?" she asked Austen.

Austen explained that he had already checked all of the animal shelters. He was planning to go back now and check again. He was hoping that someone would still find Bingo and turn him in. Next, he was planning on hanging up the "missing dog" flyers all around town.

"We can help with that," offered Evangeline.

"That sounds like a good plan," Giselle nodded in agreement. "I should probably get your phone number," Giselle said shyly. "Ya know in case we find out anything about Bingo."

"My number's on the flyer and so is my address," said Austen as he picked up his skateboard. "But I should definitely get your number."

Austen handed his phone to Giselle who smiled as she typed in her number. He thanked the girls and took off on his skateboard.

Once Austen was out of sight, Giselle dropped to the floor, freaking out. She was breathing so fast she felt like she was going to faint. She put her head between her knees. "What was I thinking? Why did I say we could help find his dog? We don't know how to find things," wheezed out Giselle between breaths.

Mercedes looked over, annoyed, and held up her phone. "Wait. What? Then how am I gonna pay for these awesome new shoes?" On screen was her favorite online clothing store. "He's gonna give us $500, remember?"

Evangeline protested, "What are you afraid of, Giselle? We know how to find things." She reached into her pocket and pulled out a wad of chewed up gum, then popped it in her mouth. "I found this tasty treat under the snack table. It still tastes minty!"

Giselle calmed down and looked at her. "Gross!"

Mercedes stared with love in her eyes at the shoes on her phone. She looked back to Giselle. "Can't you just figure this out, you know, do your boring smart thing... like when you do your homework?"

Giselle started to relax and think clearly.

"You're right Mercedes. We can do this. It's just like my George Washington report. He was able to form a secret network of spies, so we can definitely find one little puppy. We just have to make a plan. Let's write out a list of clues and suspects."

Mercedes squealed, "Exactly! Uh, what's a suspect?"

Giselle responded patiently, "A suspect is a person you think might have had something to do with the dog being missing. Kind of like when my lip gloss was missing and even though you said you didn't take it you were the only one in the room where I left it. Which made you the only suspect!"

"You never proved I took it," taunted Mercedes.

Giselle muttered under her breath, "Which is why you're still a suspect and a sneaky liar."

Evangeline was not interested in being bored by the same lip gloss argument. The last one had gone on for over a month, so she quickly stepped in to change the subject.

"We told Austen we would help find Bingo. So what do we need to do first?"

"Well, according to what I learned for my essay, we need to look for clues. A lot of times the biggest clue comes from something that you would never guess," explained Giselle. She pulled out her essay, ready to share what she had learned about spies.

Evangeline blurted out, "So is this piece of gum I found a clue?"

"What? No," Giselle said. "And spit that out! It's gross! There are millions of germs on that."

Mercedes interrupted her, "I'm not feeling all of these steps. Too boring. Goodbye perfect pair of shoes." She kissed her phone screen.

Giselle rolled her eyes and said, "I see that once again all the work falls on me."

"Hey, I just got an idea," Mercedes said. "Maybe we don't find Rainbow, but we find another dog that looks like him. There's a bunch of dogs here for the auditions."

Giselle didn't quite understand Mercedes' point, but she was glad she was trying to help.

Mercedes excitedly continued, "We find another gray and white husky, we lie to the cute boy, and we tell him it's his dog. He gets a new best friend. I get my shoes. Case closed!"

"That's terrible. You can't just replace someone you love. What if I replaced you?" Giselle said to Mercedes.

Evangeline simply said, "Easy come easy

go." She could feel another fight coming so she sat down and started watching videos on her phone.

This time Giselle couldn't hide how troubled she was. "Your plan is totally sneaky and wrong. Austen knows his dog. And his name is Bingo, not Bongo or Rainbow. Plus his dog does tricks that only he can do," said Giselle.

"And we need him for Mom and Dad's commercial," said Evangeline as she watched a video on Bingo's channel. "Subscribed!"

Giselle pointed to the video of Bingo and Austen. "We can't lie to a dog about his cute boy. I mean lie to a cute boy about how cute he is. I mean how cute his dog is."

Evangeline and Mercedes laughed hard because Giselle's tongue kept getting twisted.

"Quit laughing! You know what I mean!" shouted Giselle.

"I don't even know why you're talking about bad guys or suspects or whatever," said Mercedes. "The boy said his dog was 'missing.' Everyone knows that means it ran away. Duh. I think that your essay on spies is making you a little crazy."

Giselle paused with a, "Hmmm." She thought hard. Maybe Mercedes was right. She had been working a lot on her report lately. It was possible she had become a little too obsessed with spies.

"I mean who would want to steal a dog anyway?" Mercedes asked. "I seriously don't understand why people think it's fun to pick up poop."

Giselle didn't know what to do. She looked over Evangeline's shoulder and watched the video of Austen and Bingo on her phone. Austen's heavenly voice was very distracting.

"Okay, that's it. We're doing this my way," said Mercedes as she looked around at all the dogs. "One of these has to work." She started to walk over to a group of dogs.

"Stop!" yelled Giselle at Evangeline.

Mercedes thought she was talking to her, so she stopped and turned around.

"Pause the video. Scroll down to the comments," Giselle commanded.

Evangeline scrolled down slightly. There was a very mean, very recent comment from a user named "Hollywoof Dogs." The comment read:

THIS DOG WAS TRAINED AT OUR CENTER AND WE WERE NEVER PAID. SEND US OUR MONEY OR YOU'LL BE

SORRY.

Maybe Bingo wasn't just missing. And maybe Giselle wasn't crazy after all. She just might have found a suspect that wanted to harm Bingo. Her eyes grew wide in shock as she realized, "Bingo isn't missing... He was PUP-NAPPED!"

CHAPTER 3

The auditions finally ended and the sisters were back at home trying to crack the case. They decided their clubhouse in the backyard was the perfect place to talk. This way their mom and dad wouldn't hear them. Even though what they were doing wasn't wrong, they didn't want their parents to worry.

"I've been kidnapped before. It's no big deal," said Evangeline with a shrug.

Giselle looked at her with shock. "What are you talking about? When were you ever kidnapped?"

Evangeline continued, "Back in preschool. Just like you. Don't you remember taking kid naps? So really, we've all been kidnapped before."

Giselle couldn't tell if Evangeline was making a joke or not. She did not have time to

31

ask. Mom was going to call them in for dinner any minute.

"The person who left that mean comment pup-napped this dog," Giselle said holding up the flyer Austen gave them. "We have to figure out who it is." The thought of Austen caused her to let out a happy sigh.

Mercedes chimed in, "I agree! And we need to film ourselves when we rescue the dog from the evil kidnapper. It will make a great video for our fans! Just imagine how many views we'll get!

Mercedes clapped excitedly. She pulled out her phone and practiced posing for the victory pictures she would post when they found the dog.

"We agreed to find a missing dog. Not be action heroes in a movie where we rescue a kidnapped dog!" Giselle said sternly.

"But what about my video?" whined Mercedes.

Evangeline interrupted the argument, or conversation, or whatever it was that Mercedes and Giselle were having. She shoved her phone in their faces.

"Check out this website. I tracked down the guy who left the mean comment on Bingo's video. His name is Harold Farnblatt and he runs a dog school in Hollywood called Hollywoof Dog Studio," said Evangeline.

"Look!" Giselle exclaimed. "It's a picture of Bingo right there on the front page. And a link to Austen's channel."

Evangeline read the website out loud, "We trained this famous dog and we can train yours."

"He's totally the bad guy!" shouted Mercedes. "I mean look at him. How can he help anyone get famous? He obviously dyed his hair with some at-home box kit. Seriously! Look how streaky and faded it is. And don't even get me started on his wardrobe. Plaid shorts with a Hawaiian shirt? Yuck!"

"Mercedes you can't say someone is guilty because you think they need fashion advice," scolded Giselle. "You need evidence and proof. Didn't you listen when I was reading my essay?"

"Here's my proof," said Mercedes with a wave of her hand. "Harold Farnblatt totally sounds like a criminal name to me. Don't you agree Evangeline?"

"Maybe that's why he turned to a life of crime," realized Evangeline, suddenly agreeing with Mercedes. Evangeline stood up to act out her theory. "He didn't want to be a criminal, but his parents forced him to join the family business stealing dogs. He tried to quit, but his parents wouldn't let him. They told him, "You were born a Farnblatt and that's what Farnblatts do. Now start stealing dogs or you're out of the family!"

"It's sad really," said Mercedes with a fake sniffle.

"Can you guys focus for like two seconds?" said Giselle, obviously annoyed with them.

"Probably not," answered Evangeline.

"Where's the fun in that?" Mercedes chimed in with a giggle.

Mercedes could always tell when Giselle was about to break, so she decided to stop teasing her. "Okay okay, we're done!" Mercedes promised. "But what if I'm right and this horribly dressed, streaky-haired man is guilty? How do we prove it?"

"That's obvious," Evangeline stated. "We sneak inside and see if he has Bingo."

"That's called breaking and entering. And it's a crime. They put you in jail for that!" Giselle said in horror.

"Well if you want to do it the boring way I

guess we can go with plan B," Evangeline said as she pointed to the website. It read:

NEW AUDITION CLASS STARTS TOMORROW! SIGN UP YOUR DOG TODAY.

"What?" Mercedes gasped. "A class for auditioning? I call dibs. It's perfect! We can find little Bingbang and I can pick up a few acting tips at the same time! Yay!"

"Mercedes, it's a class for dogs," said Giselle.

"Seriously?" whined Mercedes. "Why are dogs getting all the attention right now? They're like ruining my whole life."

"Do we know anyone who has a dog?" asked Giselle. "Maybe we could borrow it?"

"I could ask Mom and Dad to get us a dog. I'll use my super cute please-I-really-want-it-face," offered Evangeline as she flashed her best cute smile.

"I know!" squealed Mercedes. "Giselle can pretend to be a dog! Her hair needs a trim so bad she could easily pass for a shaggy dog."

That was it. Mercedes had pushed Giselle too far. Giselle lunged toward her, but instead, she missed her and hit the floor.

Quickly, Mercedes jumped to her feet and ran out the clubhouse door. Within seconds Giselle was chasing Mercedes around the backyard. Everyone in the whole neighborhood could hear Mercedes screaming at the top of her lungs.

Evangeline didn't miss a beat. She grabbed her phone, headed outside, and started filming the fight. She spoke seriously, acting for the camera. "It's time for another episode of Sister Wars! What happens when one sister insults the other sister's hair? We're about to find out. Emotions are running high. Who will win this epic battle?"

Both Mercedes and Giselle stopped their argument and stared at Evangeline who was still filming them. "What do you think you're doing?" asked Giselle.

"Filming a video," answered Evangeline. "It's great. You both look really crazy so just keep going. The fans are going to love it. Now, fight to the death!"

Mercedes and Giselle looked at each other with puzzled faces.

"Get her!" yelled Mercedes.

Giselle reached for Evangeline's phone, but Evangeline wouldn't let go. Evangeline continued to film as Mercedes tried to wrestle it from her grip.

Evangeline darted around the yard. She

hid behind fruit trees, leaped over shrubs, and dodged her sisters at every turn. She held the camera over her shoulder and filmed them as they chased her.

"You will not be posting that!" ordered Giselle.

"Oh yeah, you gotta catch me to stop me!" taunted Evangeline.

The sisters screamed as they chased after Evangeline who refused to stop filming. The noise caught the attention of their dad. None of them noticed him standing in the backyard.

"Girls!" he finally yelled.

They froze in their tracks. There was a brief moment of silence, and then more complaining.

"Evangeline is trying to post a video we said not to," whined Mercedes.

"They're attacking me Dad. You saw it. This video is my evidence," Evangeline begged.

"My sisters aren't listening to me and Mercedes made fun of my hair again!" complained Giselle.

Dad whistled loudly. They stopped talking. "Girls, remember what Mom and I told you about being the GEM Sisters. It means you're a team. So, when you make videos you need to agree and work together. Right?"

"But Dad, we're not making videos for GEM Sisters," explained Mercedes. "We were looking for evidence until Giselle went crazy.

"Evidence? For what?" asked Dad.

Mercedes started to answer. She didn't notice her sisters' eyes had grown so wide they were about to pop out of their heads. Before she could say more, Evangeline interrupted.

"You're right Dad as always. Sorry. I'll delete the video," said Evangeline as she pressed the delete button on her phone. "See? All gone. Like it never happened."

Giselle could tell that Dad still had questions about what was really going on. She quickly changed the subject. "What's that you're holding?" she asked.

Dad looked down at the fancy dog collar in his hand. "Oh you are going to love this," he said.

Giselle breathed a sigh of relief as Dad showed them the collar.

"Look! It goes on like any other dog collar, but it has an ultra HD camera in it," he said excitedly. "Do you know what that means?"

The girls stood in silence waiting for each other to answer. This pretty much happened every time Dad talked about his latest favorite gadget.

Dad continued, unaffected, "We can now film a dog's eye view! Isn't that amazing?"

They all looked at him, puzzled and not impressed.

"For the commercial, I can put the viewers inside the mind of a dog. I can show people what dogs see and how they think. It's going to change the way dog treat commercials are filmed," Dad said.

For once Giselle actually wanted to hear what Dad had to say. "Can you see the signal on your phone like a security camera?" asked Giselle.

"You sure can," said Dad beaming with pride. He quickly installed a special app on Giselle's phone. "Look. You can have the live footage record right onto your phone."

Mercedes and Evangeline didn't understand why Giselle was so excited about Dad's new gadget.

"So it sends a signal through WiFi? Cool," said Giselle as she tested the app.

"I know, right?" said Dad with a smile. "Who wants to try out the collar? Mercedes, you like jewelry don't you?"

Mercedes looked back at Dad with horror.

"I said I wanted to be in the commercial, but pretend to be a dog? Absolutely not. That is beneath me!"

Dad turned to Evangeline, "What about you kiddo?'

Evangeline eyed the can of dog treats in Dad's other hand. "We'll do it!" she said happily.

"We?" answered Dad.

"My tummy and me. We agreed. We will do anything for bacon," Evangeline said, motioning to the organic bacon treat can.

Dad read the ingredient label on the can, "Hmm, just bacon, soy, and some natural flavoring… and they are organic. And more importantly, Mom's not here. Deal!"

Evangeline reached out for the treats. Dad scolded her like a dog.

"No. No. Bad doggie. Dogs can't use their hands!" said Dad. He motioned for her to get down on her hands and knees.

Dad slipped the collar on Evangeline's neck. He poured the dog treats into a bowl. He stepped behind Giselle and looked at the video on her phone.

"Take twenty doggie steps back," directed Dad, "and action!"

Giselle and Dad watched as the collar

camera showed the dog's eye view on Giselle's phone. It worked. Evangeline walked across the yard to the bowl like a dog. Cool!

Then it got not-so-cool. Evangeline slobbered and spilled food out of her mouth as she ate. More drool than cool. Kinda gross actually.

Suddenly the camera showed Mercedes' face poking into the frame.

"What's that puppy?" acted out Mercedes in front of the camera. "You need an amazingly beautiful actress to feed you dog treats for the commercial? And you think I should do it? Why thank you!"

"Cut" screamed Dad. "No overacting on my set!"

"But Dad, I can do it just like that for the commercial!" yelled Mercedes across the yard.

"You had your chance. It's NOT about you," said Dad.

"I don't understand," Mercedes replied. "Everything is about me!"

The camera signal went black on Giselle's phone.

"Bummer. The camera ran out of batteries," said Dad. "I'll go get some more. Oh and I'll get the dog costume we used for that stuffed animal commercial we did last month. I want to see

41

Evangeline catch a frisbee in her mouth. It's gonna be incredible! Be right back."

"Can't wait," shouted Giselle with excitement. When Dad was safely in the house, she motioned for her sisters to huddle together.

"This camera is exactly what we need to find Bingo! Austen is going to love me... I mean love us when we find his dog," said Giselle.

'How is the camera going to help us find a dog?' asked Mercedes.

Before Giselle could answer Mom yelled out the back door. "Girls! Time to eat. I made healthy spinach tacos. I used spinach instead of meat. You're gonna love it!"

"Oh yum," Mercedes lied with a smile.

"Be right in," Giselle said as Mom went back inside the house.

Evangeline frowned and grabbed the rest of the organic bacon treats. She offered them to her sisters, who considered the choice then shook their heads no.

"More for me," said Evangeline.

Giselle stopped them just before they went inside. "Listen. I've got a plan. After school tomorrow we're going to Hollywoof Dog Studio, and we're going to prove that Harold Farnblatt stole Bingo!"

CHAPTER 4

The GEM Sisters were standing outside
arguing. The Hollywoof Dog Studio was an
old run down brick building surrounded by a
tall rusty chain link fence. The sound of dogs
barking echoed from inside.

"I said no!" Mercedes hissed.

Giselle held up a cute fuzzy dog costume
she had borrowed from her dad. Well more like
borrowed without permission. Giselle planned
to return both the costume and the collar
camera once they had their proof.

"C'mon Mercedes. The only way we can
film inside without being noticed is for you to
dress up like a dog and wear the collar," begged
Giselle.

"Absolutely not!" said Mercedes. "I am an
actress not an animal. And I'm having an
amazing hair day."

Mercedes threw the costume on the ground. She pulled out her phone and scrolled through her social media pretending not to listen.

"We need to see if Bingo is here," continued Giselle. "I've got it all planned out. Evangeline will act cute and ask tons of questions to distract the owner. That way you, dressed as the dog, can sneak around and look for clues. Meanwhile I'll record the whole thing on my phone."

"You think Evangeline can do 'cute' better than me? I've never been so insulted!" yelled Mercedes. "No offense Evangeline."

Evangeline didn't respond. She wasn't listening to her sisters argue. They competed a lot and to be honest she got bored by their fights. Instead Evangeline was focused on the barking dogs inside. Since she spoke "dog" she knew their barks were cries for help and she needed to take action.

"You want me to dress up like a dog because I made fun of your hair yesterday," Mercedes continued to argue.

Giselle was about to fight back when Evangeline interrupted.

"Arf! Arf!" barked Evangeline.

Mercedes and Giselle looked over.

Evangeline was wearing the dog costume. She was down on her hands and knees trying to open a can of bacon treats. Having fuzzy paws instead of hands made it difficult to open the lid.

"No no no!" yelled Giselle.

"Why not?" asked Mercedes. "She totally looks the part."

"I mean no more dog treats," lectured Giselle. "Give me those." She took the can of treats. Evangeline barked angrily.

"Stop it! Quiet!" ordered Giselle. Evangeline didn't obey. She continued to bark faster and louder.

"Just give her a treat," ordered Mercedes. "Dad did it yesterday."

Giselle gave in and popped a bacon treat into Evangeline's mouth. Evangeline ate it quickly then licked Giselle's hand to say thank you. Then she rolled on her back wanting her belly to be scratched.

"Never in a million, billion years," said Giselle as she opened the door to the Hollywoof Studio. "Okay you two follow my lead and try to stay out of trouble."

The girls took less than two steps inside the building before the terrible smell hit them.

Yesterday they had been around lots of dogs at the auditions, but those dogs had been bathed and groomed to look their best. This place was strange. They could smell and hear loud dogs barking, but they didn't see any dogs.

At the front desk sat the owner Harold Farnblatt. Mercedes wasn't sure what offended her more, the smell or his outfit. He wore a faded Hawaiian shirt with ugly checkered golf pants and mismatched socks with sandals. He smelled just awful, like a mix of mothballs and taco chips.

Mercedes whispered to her sisters, "Ew! He smells even worse than he looks."

Giselle shushed Mercedes. She walked up to the counter and gave a dazzling smile.

"Quiet!" yelled Harold at the top of his lungs. The sisters all jumped at the sound of his voice. Next he let out a loud, long whistle. Within seconds the dogs stopped barking from behind the door next to them.

Harold turned to the girls and smiled. "Why hello young ladies. How can I help you today?"

Giselle and Mercedes didn't know how to respond. This guy definitely seemed a little crazy.

"Arf!" barked Evangeline answering for

them.

Harold looked down to see Evangeline dressed as a dog. "What's with the dog outfit?" he asked. His face grew puzzled as he watched her stuff several bacon treats in her mouth.

"Sshhh," Giselle commanded. "Please don't say that too loud. You see, our sister doesn't realize she's a girl. I mean, she thinks she's a girl dog. What I'm trying to say is she gets up everyday and dresses like a dog," she stuttered, trying to make up the story as she went.

Both Mercedes and Harold had confused looks on their faces as Giselle continued to talk. Mercedes knew Giselle was a terrible liar, but this was a disaster.

"By get up I mean, she rolls off her... dog bed. Because she doesn't, like, sleep in a human bed of course. Because that would be normal. Then she gets out of the shower and puts on this dog costume... instead of normal clothes. Well, not a shower, a dog bath..."

Mercedes knew Giselle was about to ruin everything. So she jumped in with dramatic flair. "What my rambling older sister is trying to say, is that our dear sweet little sister had a heartbreaking, tragic accident."

Instantly huge tears welled up in Mercedes'

eyes and rolled unchecked down her cheeks. All eyes were on her. Even Evangeline stopped eating to hear the story.

"Our sister had just gotten a brand new bike for her birthday. It was a stormy day and our mom begged her not to go outside. You could see storm clouds coming, but she didn't care. She just wanted to ride her new bike. She ran out of the house so quick she forgot her helmet."

Mercedes gasped for dramatic effect and continued.

"Before she knew it the storm was practically chasing her. She pedaled faster and faster! She was going so fast down the hill she didn't see the lightening behind her... CRASH!"

Harold Farnblatt's mouth gaped open. He wanted to know what happened next. Giselle tried to step in, but Mercedes glared. She didn't want Giselle ruining her award-winning performance.

"The lightening hit her and knocked her off the bike. She hit her head so hard on the ground all the doctors said she was lucky to be alive. When she finally woke up in the hospital she could only bark. The doctors say her brain thinks she's a dog."

Harold Farnblatt gasped and held his hands to his mouth. "That's so terrible. The poor dear."

Giselle was shocked he was believing Mercedes' story. She was sure any minute he was going to throw them out. Then they would never get inside to look for Bingo.

Mercedes continued, "We were told to raise her as a dog. So now our family is doing everything we can to help her. It's a rare medical condition with no known cure, it's called um, um..."

Oh no. Mercedes knew how to perform, but memorizing science vocabulary words was not her talent. Giselle came to the rescue.

"Dog-a-lo-pop-lee-us," explained Giselle. "It's so rare she's the first human to have a medical study written about her. And that is why we are here. For training." Giselle leaned in closer to Harold and whispered, "Especially training to stop her from peeing all over the floor. It's a real problem."

Evangeline barked loudly. She stuck out her tongue. Harold glanced down. He was struck by her cuteness. "Well if she has to be a dog, at least we can make sure she's well-trained. What's her name so I can sign her up?"

Giselle and Mercedes looked at each other. Since they were undercover they didn't want to give Evangeline's real name, but neither one of them could think of a dog name. The girls looked to Evangeline who was licking the now empty can of bacon treats.

"Bacon!" shouted Mercedes. "We call her Bacon because it's the one word she still seems to understand."

"Arf arf!" responded Evangeline as she rolled happily on her back.

Harold motioned for the girls to go through the gate. "Training starts in the room at the end of the hall in ten minutes."

The sisters walked quickly down the hall before their luck could change.

"I knew I could trick him with my acting skills," laughed Mercedes.

"Well thanks for jumping in," said Giselle. "You really saved us. Honestly, it's kind of scary how good you are at lying."

Mercedes smiled. "Hello? Actress!" she said pointing to herself. "Don't worry, I won't forget about you when I'm famous."

Before the girls went through the door, Giselle turned to Evangeline. "You have to use real words so we can work together. Remember why we're here. To find Bingo. Okay?"

Evangeline growled for a second then answered, "Fine. But let me ask the questions to the dogs. I'm the only one of us who can speak 'dog', remember?" She held out her paw. "A little more bacon please. I saw the other can in your backpack."

Giselle shook her head no and pushed Evangeline through the door. The large room was poorly lit. The light blue paint on the walls was stained from years of dogs peeing on it. Gross!

"I see why he needs to kidnap dogs for money," said Mercedes. "This place is a dump."

Giselle noticed the framed picture of Bingo hanging on the wall. Above the picture was a giant gold star. Sure Harold may have been nice, but this proved he was still a suspect. The girls didn't know where to start looking for clues. They walked over to the group of dog owners and began to chat.

Evangeline ran to play with the other dogs. In her excitement she didn't see what the dogs were doing until it was too late. The dogs were all sniffing each other's behinds and licking each other's faces. Evangeline got nose to nose with a small rat terrier, who began licking her face.

"I'm all for the face licking, but that's it. Got it?" warned Evangeline.

The dog looked at her confused. "Oh," she thought, "I'm speaking human." Evangeline repeated what she had said, but this time with barking.

The rat terrier stuck his short stubby tail in the air and farted right in her face.

"Ew! You've had way too many dog treats," Evangeline said, using her paw to hold her nose. The rat terrier scampered away, scared of the weird talking dog.

Harold Farnblatt entered the room. Dogs and owners got quiet as he began to speak. "Ladies and gentleman. Or should I say Labradors and German Shepherds." He chuckled. He loved that joke.

"His jokes are worse than Dad's," Mercedes muttered to Giselle.

"I'm sure you've all seen the online videos starring this dog," Harold continued. He pointed to the framed picture of Bingo on the wall. "I trained this dog to be a superstar, and I can train your dogs too."

A plump pit bull interrupted Harold's speech barking loudly. Harold responded to the dog as if he understood him.

"Why yes. Bingo my good pal was just here yesterday," replied Harold with a sneaky smile. "He said he's planning on coming back soon to help me teach some classes because he couldn't have done it without me."

"Did he really understand what that dog said?" asked Mercedes. "Because I thought Evangeline was just pretending to speak 'dog.'"

Giselle rolled her eyes. "He said Bingo was here yesterday. But Austen told us yesterday that Bingo was missing. So, either Harold is lying or he's keeping Bingo here. We need to distract Harold so Evangeline can snoop around."

Harold continued his long-winded speech, "When your dogs graduate they will jump higher, listen better, and impress your friends and neighbors."

One shy little girl raised her hand. Harold ignored it.

"No need for questions. They will all be answered as we proceed through the training. Now who wants to have a famous dog?"

Everyone raised their hands except for Giselle. She looked over to Mercedes whose hand was waving excitedly.

"Okay then, quiet down," said Harold. "First lesson, teaching your dog to sit."

The dogs all gathered in a circle with their owners seated beside them. All of them except for Evangeline. She was being a very pesky dog. Her floppy dog ears kept whacking Mercedes in the face. She couldn't sit still.

Mercedes snapped at her, "Bad dog. Calm down. Sit down! You're ruining my hair!"

Evangeline liked playing the troublemaking dog. "Arf! Arf Arf!" she taunted. She ran circles around Mercedes causing Harold to come over.

Giselle quickly pushed record on her phone. The collar camera around Evangeline's neck was live! They were going to prove Harold Farnblatt was guilty! Giselle pointed to the collar and gave Mercedes a secret wink.

Mercedes spoke up. "Mr. Harold sir, I feel bad for my sister, but I simply can't take anymore! Can you make her stop?"

Harold got down on one knee and looked straight into Evangeline's eyes. Then he spoke in a gentle yet firm voice. "Sit," he commanded.

Evangeline found her body unable to resist. She melted to the floor, her knees no longer able to hold her up. She sat very still, but kept barking loudly. This guy had mind powers.

"No barking," he said in a serious voice. Harold stuck out his long pointer finger.

Evangeline stopped barking. She was powerless against his strong gaze. Mercedes couldn't believe how commanding this poorly dressed man was.

Just as Evangeline was about to bark again, Harold pointed to the can of dog treats. He motioned for Giselle to hold out the treat in front of Evangeline's nose. "Quiet," he said in a firm, calm voice.

When Harold was sure she was going to stay quiet, he broke his gaze with her and told Giselle to give her the dog treat. The excited class clapped loudly. Harold took a bow.

Giselle quickly turned to her sisters. It was go time. "Mercedes get ready to distract Harold. Evangeline, wag your tail like you have to pee."

"Harold! Help!" Giselle shouted, "My sister looks like she's going to do that thing I told you about earlier."

Harold did not understand. Giselle pointed to Evangeline wagging her tail. When he still didn't get what she was trying to say, Giselle crossed her legs and started jumping up and down. By now the whole class was staring at her.

"Listen! She's about to add another stain to your wall. Can you tell me where the restroom is?" asked Giselle.

Harold explained the bathroom was down the hall last door on the left. He told her three times to only go to the door on the left NOT the door on the right. Giselle wondered why he kept repeating himself. She figured he had something to hide.

"Mercedes you keep taking notes about the training. I don't want to miss a thing," Giselle said loudly so everyone could hear. She then whispered to Mercedes as they walked away, "Keep him distracted."

Mercedes nodded yes as the two of them left. She a took a deep breath and thought of what she was going to do with her reward money. "New shoes. New shoes. New shoes," she repeated to herself. Then she yelled to Harold who was now on the other side of the room. "Can I help you Mr. Harold? I just love working with these beautiful smelly animals," lied Mercedes.

Out in the hallway, Giselle informed Evangeline that they were going to find out what was behind the door on the right. Harold was hiding something in that room. Bingo was probably one of the dogs making all of those barking noises when they first came in the building.

When they got to the door Harold said not to enter, Giselle tried to turn the handle. It was locked.

That's when Evangeline pointed to the doggie door. "I can fit in that," she said proudly.

"I'm not letting you go inside there by yourself," said Giselle.

"I'll be fine," explained Evangeline. "I'll look around and you can watch everything on your phone."

Giselle started pacing. She always paced when she couldn't decide what to do. It was a good plan, but what if she got hurt? Giselle decided it wasn't worth the risk. She looked down to tell her sister no, but she was gone!

"Wow! It's really dark in here," said Evangeline's voice on the phone. "No wonder all these dogs are barking. I'd be scared too if I was locked up like this."

Giselle jolted down and poked her head inside the doggie door. "Get back here now!"

"No. I'm looking for Bingo. It will only take a second," explained Evangeline. She reached through the doggie door, "Now hand over the bacon treats."

"This is not the time for a snack," scolded Giselle.

"It's not for me," explained Evangeline. "I'm going to use the treats to get Bingo to follow me out."

Giselle was impressed with Evangeline's plan. She passed the can of treats through the doggie door. Mercedes' voice filled the hallway.

"Oh no! I think Harold's coming," she said. "I'm watching you on my phone. If anything goes wrong get out of there as fast as you can!"

Giselle kicked the doggie door shut and quickly stood outside the bathroom door on the other side of the hallway. She was right. Harold was coming to check on them and Mercedes was talking extra loud as a warning.

"Oh look. There's my sister," shouted Mercedes.

"Everything okay out here?" asked Harold. His eyes darted to the door on the right. He looked down at the doggie door which he noticed was cracked open. Harold took a step toward the door and put his hand on the doorknob.

In a panic Giselle grabbed Harold's arm. "It's amazing! Whatever you did is already working. Our sister is in the bathroom using the toilet! Thank you!" she said excitedly.

Harold got an awkward look on his face. "Well good I guess. But I think you all had better get back to class."

"It's number two," Giselle whispered. "And it smells pretty bad in there. How about we go back to class with you and I come check on her in a little bit. I can't wait to learn more!"

"Me too!" Mercedes chimed in, playing along.

Giselle and Mercedes each grabbed one of Harold's arms and walked him back to the room where everyone was waiting. Harold began teaching again while the sisters sneakily peeked at the live recording on Giselle's phone. Evangeline was in a room full of cages.

"It must be like a pet hotel," whispered Giselle to Mercedes. "A place where people keep their dogs overnight when they go on vacation."

Evangeline opened cage after cage to look inside. Almost every cage had a dog, but none of the dogs were huskies.

"Bingo," sang Evangeline. "Oh Bingo, where are you? I have a treat for you." She cracked opened the can. The smell of bacon filled the air.

The dogs barked eagerly wanting the yummy

treat. The sound echoed through Hollywoof Dog Studio until it reached Harold. "What's going on out in the hall?" he asked.

"I'm sure it's nothing," lied Giselle in a panic.

"Oh it's definitely something," Harold said, very upset.

Giselle looked down at the screen, but it went black. Oh no! The collar had run out of batteries.

Harold walked out into the hall. Giselle and Mercedes quickly followed. All of a sudden Evangeline ran past them. She was on two feet, sprinting and throwing dog treats up in the air. Mercedes and Giselle looked at each other. Where was she going?

Mercedes yelled after her little sister, "Halt! Sit! Bad puppy!"

Then Giselle saw why Evangeline was running. She panicked and grabbed Mercedes by the shoulder. Mercedes turned. A pack of dogs had burst out of the doggie door. They were running down the hallway as fast as they could. They wanted Evangeline's dog treats!

Harold stood like a rock. He put one hand in the air with a stop sign pose. "Heel. I said heel!" Harold shouted in a booming voice to the excited pack of dogs.

As Harold whistled a Great Dane knocked him over. All of the dogs followed, making a path straight across his chest. Giselle and Mercedes saw they were going to get trampled next.

"Oh no! The dogs have gone savage," shouted Giselle.

Mercedes screamed at the top of her lungs, "RUN for your life!"

CHAPTER 5

The girls stepped off a city bus holding their noses. Their feet hit the sidewalk and they all took a deep breath of fresh air. Mercedes reached into her backpack and pulled out a bottle of perfume. She sprayed herself from head to toe.

"That bus smelled worse than the dog place!" whined Mercedes. "I need a shower!"

Giselle looked down at her phone. On the screen was a map. She compared the map to the neighborhood around them. She looked at street signs and house numbers. "This way," she said motioning her sisters to follow.

The sisters walked a short while and arrived at a little yellow house with a dark green door. Giselle compared the house number to the address on the flyer Austen had given them. "Maybe I should have texted that we were coming?" she said nervously.

Bang! Bang! Bang! Too late. Mercedes had already knocked on the door. "Hello? Dog boy?" she shouted.

Giselle considered running. Her heart was racing. Before she could decide Austen answered the door. "Oh hey. You again. You're those sisters, right?" he asked.

"We're the GEM Sisters," said Mercedes clearly annoyed that he had forgotten.

"Where's the little one?" questioned Austen.

Mercedes pointed to Evangeline who was sniffing a flower in the front yard. She was still wearing the dog costume.

Evangeline noticed a fly near the flower and began to hit it with her paw. The fly buzzed around her face and then flew into her mouth. Her eyes grew wide then she spit it out. "That tickled," she said giggling.

"She's one weird little kid, isn't she?" asked Austen.

"You have no idea," Giselle said to him with a smile. "Sorry to stop by without texting. We just wanted to give you an update about Bingo."

"You found him!" Austen said excitedly as he gave Giselle a big hug.

She considered lying and saying yes so the

hug could last forever. "Sorry no," she answered and slowly pulled herself back. "We've got good news and bad news."

"Harold Farnblatt did not steal BenBen!" Mercedes exclaimed.

"She means Bingo," Giselle corrected, annoyed at Mercedes for saying the wrong name again.

"Harold Farnblatt?" Austen said confused. "Why do you think he would take Bingo?"

"Obviously the guy looks like a criminal and he smells guilty too," Mercedes stated then folded her arms. "But we don't think he's a suspect anymore."

Giselle could see by Austen's confused face that they weren't explaining things well. "We know that you said Bingo was missing and you thought that he had run away, but then Evangeline saw this horrible comment Harold left on your video. So we thought maybe he pup-napped your dog to get back the money he says you owe him."

Mercedes gasped at the memory, "And that place is a total dump by the way, seriously disgusting. Ew! We checked everywhere and then we accidentally let out a bunch of dogs who almost killed us."

"But anyway," said Giselle not wanting to tell that part of the story. "We didn't find Bingo there. Now we know it was just us blowing the whole thing up in our imagination. Bingo probably just wandered off somewhere so we thought we could come help you look."

Austen stood there with a puzzled look on his face. "Actually, you guys are right," he said as he reached his hand into his pocket. "This was in my mailbox when I got home from school today."

He pulled out a crumpled piece of paper and handed it to Giselle. The light yellow paper was ripped and had a sticky black spot on the bottom. There was a note written in blue marker that read:

THE DOG IS SAFE WITH ME. STOP LOOKING FOR HIM!

"We were right!" said Mercedes excitedly. "He was pup-napped!" Mercedes busted into a victory dance. She stopped when she noticed Giselle was glaring at her.

Giselle looked closer at the top right corner of the paper, "Guys check it out. It looks like there was a picture here that was ripped off. You can see it had some sort of rounded edge kind of like a circle."

Evangeline approached the group to get a closer look. She smelled the paper in Giselle's hand. She sniffed quickly like a dog would. She took a big long sniff of the black spot on the paper. Then she stuck out her tongue and licked it!

"Not chocolate like I thought," she gagged. Then she licked again. "It tastes kind of like the chemicals we use to clean the bathroom." Evangeline stuck out her tongue which now had a light black color. "Cool. Look at my tongue!"

"Gross! Go rinse out your mouth!" ordered Giselle.

"Does Bingo have a water dish out here?" Evangeline asked Austen. He nodded yes.

Austen walked with Evangeline to the large tree in the front yard. There were several dog toys around a small water bowl. "This is where we were practicing for the audition the day he disappeared."

Evangeline sniffed the bowl on the ground. It was still filled halfway with water. There was a layer of dirt at the bottom. She paused, took a deep breath, and then stuck her tongue into the water lapping it up like a dog.

Giselle was about to stop Evangeline but didn't. She decided to focus on what to do next.

"There MUST be a clue that we are missing," she announced to the group. Giselle loved it in movies when someone said something like that and WHAM! Another person thought of something great. But nothing happened. Everyone stared at her. Awkward.

"This is so boring!" said Mercedes. "Listen I'm sorry about your dog, but I kind of thought we'd find him by now. Probably best to just say goodbye and get a new one."

"Huh?" asked Austen, who didn't know how to react.

"What Mercedes is trying to say is she hopes you have someone you can turn to in this difficult time. A girlfriend maybe?" Giselle patted Austen on the shoulder to comfort him.

"Nah, I don't have a girlfriend. I just have Bingo. Well, had Bingo," he said trying not to get upset.

"Excellent! I mean, very helpful to know," said Giselle proud of herself for finding out the girlfriend situation.

"Arf Arf Arf!" barked Evangeline. She sounded like she was in a panic. "Arf Arf!" she barked even louder.

Austen dashed off running around the large tree. Giselle quickly followed. He pushed a branch out of his way as he rounded the corner. Giselle turned the corner just as the branch snapped back. WHACK! It hit her in the face. She swiped her finger under her nose. Good. It wasn't bleeding. Her eyes were watering from the sting.

Austen hadn't noticed and ran over to Evangeline to see what was going on.

"Arf Arf Arf!" she continued to bark.

Austen turned to see Giselle's eyes watering. "Ah Giselle. Don't cry, she's fine," he said as he draped his arm over her shoulder. "You're one super cool big sister to worry about your little sis like that."

Giselle couldn't hide her huge smile. It was the first time Austen had said her name aloud. She stood very still hoping that Austen would keep his arm there a little longer. No luck. He let go and bent down to see Evangeline. She was sniffing a newly found dog collar.

"That's Bingo's collar!" said Austen as he pulled it out of the grass. "He was wearing it the day he went missing."

"That means the kidnapper must have come in your yard. Everybody look for more clues," ordered Giselle. She reached down and petted Evangeline on the head. "Nice job!"

"If you want to find a dog, you have to think like one," Evangeline explained. She quickly licked Giselle's hand.

"Ew! Please stop doing that!" said Giselle annoyed.

"I told you. Think like a dog!" Evangeline commanded. Just then a fly buzzed by her face. She ran off to chase it.

"Mercedes! Come over here and help," shouted Giselle.

"More work?" Mercedes groaned. That was it. This whole day got worse every second. She marched up to Austen. "Listen, mister. This is not what we signed on for. If we're going to keep helping you find BoGo or BitBit, or whatever his name is, then we're going to need more money!"

"We already agreed to help," lectured Giselle. "So look for clues or ask questions, but stop complaining!"

"Ask questions?" said Mercedes with a smirk. "Fine. Austen I've got some questions. How do you get all those views? Do you post new videos every day, or just once a week? How did you decide on your video's format? What do the fans think is more important, the outfits or the accessories?" Mercedes spit-fired questions faster than Austen could answer.

Austen was caught off guard, "Woah, chillax, girl. You are like off the wall. How does any of that help me find Bingo?"

"Ha ha! She's just joking," Giselle said with a nervous laugh. She gave Mercedes a serious look and muttered under her breath, "No more questions about being internet famous. Don't ruin this for me!"

Mercedes stuck her tongue out at Giselle and stormed off. "Great idea!" yelled Giselle pretending Mercedes was listening. We definitely should get pictures of the yard. Let's look for more clues. Ok. Thanks for offering to take the photos."

Mercedes pulled out her phone and started taking pictures. Only she didn't take pictures of the yard like Giselle had asked. "Clues are dumb," Mercedes muttered annoyed. "The only thing picture worthy in this yard is me!"

Giselle tried to get the questions back on track. The sun was going down and she knew there was very little time before they had to be home for dinner. "Can you think of anyone who would want to steal Bingo?"

Austen looked down and paused. "Gosh, nobody. Cuz everyone loves him."

"Well let's keep looking for clues and hope that something turns up," Giselle said with an encouraging smile.

"Everybody!" shouted Evangeline. "I know what happened!"

They all ran over to see. "So, you and Bingo were playing together when Bingo was like 'Austen, I got an itch.' And then you scratched his belly and he was like 'oh yeah, that's the stuff.' But neither of you noticed the Squirrel King and his mob of goons. You see they were watching you the whole time."

Giselle did not like where this story was headed.

"It's a known fact that squirrels' brains are a thousand times larger than humans," Evangeline continued ignoring Giselle who was shaking her head no. "Now Austen, you didn't know it, but Bingo and the Squirrel King are sworn enemies.

"Ok. That's enough Evangeline," Giselle said.

"Then what happened?" asked Mercedes. She always loved hearing Evangeline's odd stories.

"The squirrels were sick of Bingo peeing on their favorite tree. They waited for Austen to go inside to hatch their plan for revenge. First, they threw acorns to distract Bingo. Look! Here's proof," she said holding up one she found in the yard.

"Uh that's a rock," said Austen confused.

Evangeline continued, "Then they worked together grabbing each others' tails to form a squirrel chain. They dangled down from this branch and grabbed Bingo within moments of Austen leaving. They tied him up with branches, gagged him with leaves, and pulled him up into the tree. He's still up there!"

She pointed and everyone looked up. To nothing. There was no way a dog could be hidden in the tree. Actually there weren't any squirrels either. Everyone looked at Evangeline like she was crazy.

Giselle decided she had better get her sisters away from Austen before he never wanted to see her again.

At that moment an old rusty van pulled up. It clanged and sputtered to a stop in front of Austen's house. There was a giant paw print on the side and a sign that read:

PAWS AND CLAWS GROOMING.

"Aw man I forgot to tell Jack not to come," groaned Austen.

Mercedes asked, "Who's Jack?"

"He's Bingo's groomer," said Austen. "Bingo is always wicked excited when Jack's van rumbles up. Bingo's like egg-static to get a bath and have his nails trimmed.

"What?" Mercedes shrieked. "This DOG has a mobile stylist? I don't accept this! Why is a dog getting treated better than me?"

Everyone ignored Mercedes' outburst as they watched a college-aged, shaggy-haired guy named Jack come out of the van. He was all smiles. He smelled like wet dog and his hands looked like they hadn't been washed in a year.

"He's the stylist?" Mercedes said alarmed. "Nevermind."

"Where's my favorite puppy?" asked Jack with a whistle.

"Jack! Bingo's missing. Sorry, man. I should've called to cancel, but I've been out of my mind trying to find him."

Jack's face turned to alarm. "Oh no, not Bingo. What about his big audition yesterday?"

Giselle started to answer, "Well Austen told us about his dog-"

Austen interrupted, "Oh hey, sorry, these are my friends, the GEM Sisters. They're like, trying to help me find Bingo."

"Hey girls," Jack said. "I don't know how well you know Bingo, but I wouldn't get too worried."

Giselle and Austen asked at the same time, "Why?"

Giselle blushed. *Jinx* she thought. *They were just so connected.*

Jack continued, "Think about it. Bingo has a lot of spirit, I bet he just wandered off. I've heard the neighbors just yesterday talking about puppies getting loose and running around. I bet he'll be back in a day or two when he gets homesick."

Austen wasn't so sure. "You know Bingo. He wouldn't leave like that."

"Well we don't think he's missing," Mercedes said sternly. "We think the dog was kidnapped. Where were you yesterday afternoon?"

"Kidnapped? Whoa! What's with all of the questions?" Jack asked.

Just then, Jack noticed Evangeline dressed like a dog sniffing around his van. A hose stuck out of the side. She turned on the nozzle and water poured out onto the street. Evangeline put her head under the water and took a big drink.

"Stop that!" he screamed. You can't drink my

bathwater!"

Hearing the term bathwater made Evangeline gag and spit the water out.

Jack turned off the water. He took a breath and calmed down. "Sorry to scare you. It's not that the water will hurt you. It's fresh water. It's just that I don't have extra water to waste. I've got a lot more dirty dogs to wash today."

"You have a bathtub in your van?" asked Evangeline.

"Yeah. That's what I do," said Jack. He pressed a small button on the back door by the license plate. Both of the doors popped open.

Evangeline looked inside the back of the van. Instead of seats, there was a small bathtub and lots of shelves with different supplies. It was very dirty inside. Bottles, brushes, and towels were scattered everywhere.

"So people pay you to come to their house and clean their dogs?" she asked.

"Well they don't pay a lot, but I like the job. And it's fun to hang out with dogs all day," answered Jack.

"Maybe I'll get a job like this when I grow up," said Evangeline. She reached over and grabbed a clear bottle filled with black shampoo on the floor of the van. She pretended to give herself a bath.

Mercedes quickly grabbed the bottle, "Ew! Evangeline this shampoo is for dogs. Don't touch anything else, it's super gross in there. No offense," said Mercedes as she threw the bottle back. She looked down at her hand that was now super dirty. Gross!

"It costs a lot more than you think to start a dog grooming business," Jack said to Evangeline. "You might want to start saving now."

Jack turned and put his hand on Austen's shoulder to comfort him. "Bingo's a great dog. He's smart. Trust me, he'll find his way home. I'll keep an eye out for him as I drive around the neighborhood to my other appointments."

"Uh hello, we already told you he didn't run away, he was pup-napped," said Mercedes.

"Well then I guess good luck finding whoever took him," Jack said as he got in the van. He started to drive away then stopped. "You might want to start with the neighbors. I've heard a few people complaining about dogs in this neighborhood. Ya know, too much poop left on the sidewalks."

"Do you remember who said it?" asked Giselle.

"No sorry. I'm late for my next wash. Bingo is a special dog. He'll turn up. I'm sure of it." Jack waved goodbye as he drove off.

"That's our next clue!" said Giselle excitedly. She could tell by the look on everyone's faces that they had no idea what she was thinking. "All the neighbors are suspects!"

CHAPTER 6

The GEM Sisters were on the sidewalk in front of Austen's house. They had no clue which way to go first. There were so many houses and not one of them seemed like a home for criminals. The girls thought for sure a pup-napper would live in a scary Halloween-style house. These houses looked like normal, boring homes.

Austen rode up on his skateboard wearing a helmet and carrying a hockey stick. "Sorry I can't stay and help. Like I totally want to, but my team is in the finals and they're counting on me," he said.

"Of course. Good luck. Maybe I can come watch you play sometime. I mean we. I mean my sisters and me," Giselle said with a nervous giggle.

"Can you text me if you find out anything?" asked Austen as his phone buzzed.

Giselle smiled and nodded yes.

"I'm late. Gotta go!" he said as he texted into his phone and skated away.

"Okay. Let's find this dog already and get on with our lives," Mercedes groaned. "My acting career is suffering from all this doggie detective work."

Evangeline sat down on the curb, "I wish I was a dog," she said holding her tummy. "People always give them treats so they never get hungry."

Giselle felt overwhelmed, but she was not going to let Austen down. She closed her eyes and imagined her first kiss. "Worth it," she said to herself.

She needed to form a plan, but first, she had to get Evangeline a snack. Giselle quickly pulled things out of her backpack looking for food. Her bag was full of more stuff than her locker at school. No wonder it was so heavy. As she piled things on her lap, she gave her sisters a pep talk.

"We're going to go door-to-door and question all the neighbors," she commanded. "We'll start with the house directly across the street. I figure they're the ones most likely to have seen something." Giselle spotted a single bacon dog treat in her bag. She picked it up. It was stuck to a lollipop.

"Bacon Pop? Score!" said Evangeline with a smile and started licking.

Giselle started shoving things back into her bag when Mercedes grabbed a pair of science goggles from the pile.

"Why do you have safety goggles from school?" she asked. "I mean hello, if you're going to steal stuff, you should take things actually worth stealing."

Giselle grabbed the goggles back. "These are my own personal pair. I used my allowance to pay for them. See? They have a special zoom lens in the bottom corner."

"Nerd alert!" Mercedes interrupted.

Giselle chose to ignore Mercedes and stick to her plan. "Any of these neighbors could be guilty! We need to know if they've seen the dog or not. Then we will look for clues to find out if they're lying."

"Pass!" answered Mercedes before she could finish. "I'll sit here with Evangeline and watch our stuff. You can go ask boring questions."

"Fine," said Giselle. "I'll do it myself. I don't need you guys."

She walked across the street, knocked on

the door, and glanced back at her sisters. They were ignoring her and digging through her bag. She rolled her eyes at their lack of support.

Just then the front door flew open. An older woman with short curly hair stepped out. She was wearing a striped bathrobe and smelled like fried catfish. She was wiping her hands on a black stained rag.

"What do you think you're doing? Don't you see the sign?" she asked in a raspy voice. She pointed to a sign that read:

NO TRESPASSING.

Giselle coughed at the strong smell of fish. "Excuse me ma'am. Your neighbor across the street has recently lost his dog."

The woman pointed to Austen's house. "That teen brat who's always making videos on his phone? Good! I hope his loud barky dog never comes back! I only wish he would have gone missing sooner."

SLAM! Giselle jumped back as the woman's door almost hit her in the face.

"Now get off my porch!" the woman's muffled voice yelled from inside.

She didn't know if the mean woman was a suspect or just angry. Giselle was too scared to knock again and find out.

Giselle walked back to see Mercedes giggling at her defeat. "Only fifty more houses to go sis!" said Mercedes with a mocking smile.

"You think you could do better?" asked Giselle.

"Duh. I know I can," Mercedes answered, certain of herself. "I get people to do what I want all the time. That's how I outsold everyone in my school's cookie fundraiser."

Giselle looked down the street at the long row of houses. "Care to make a bet? You and I each take a side of the street. Whoever finishes all their house interviews first, wins."

"Okay, but the loser has to clean the winner's bedroom for a month," said Mercedes as she held out her hand.

Giselle grabbed Mercedes' hand and shook it. "Evangeline you're the bet master."

"Not again," whined Evangeline. "Can't we just work together, get home early, and enjoy a yummy dinner?"

"Call it Evangeline!" ordered Mercedes.

Evangeline groaned. "Ugh. Fine! Do you both agree to the terms of this dumb bet?"

Giselle and Mercedes both answered "yes" at the same time. They dropped hands and Giselle took off running leaving Evangeline with her backpack.

Giselle was the fastest runner of the three sisters. She reached the house on her side of the street first.

"Ha slowpoke!" she yelled back to Mercedes. Giselle knocked on the front door. An elderly woman opened the door slowly and smiled. Giselle smiled back. This was gonna be a piece of cake.

Mercedes had a different plan to win. She dug through each sister's backpack pulling out different items. Evangeline's reading glasses, Giselle's notebook, a pencil, and several hair ties. "This will be even easier than the five thousand boxes of cookies I sold," she told Evangeline as she ran off.

Evangeline looked down and saw all three backpacks. "Seriously?" She lifted the heavy bags, tossed them over her shoulder, and slowly followed behind her sisters.

Mercedes ran towards her first house. She looked like a superhero putting on pieces of her costume.

Meanwhile, Giselle was struggling to carry a twenty-five pound watermelon from the elderly woman's car.

"You're such a dear for helping me," the old

woman said. "And when you're done I need a light bulb changed on my front porch."

Giselle was trying to hide that she was annoyed. "But can you tell me if you have seen the dog on the flyer I gave you?"

"I can only see shapes without my glasses," she answered. "I simply can't remember where I put them."

Giselle looked at the glasses on top of the woman's head. The only way this woman could steal a dog would be if it climbed into her car and a friendly neighbor helped carry it into her house. Sheesh!

Mercedes, back on her side of the street, now looked like a businesswoman. She wore Evangeline's reading glasses and her hair was up in a tight bun. She held a notebook and had a pencil stuck above her ear. A tall balding man answered the door.

"Good evening sir," said Mercedes in a thick southern accent. "I'm with the city and we're tracking how many people live in the houses on this block. We sent a letter."

"Oh, sorry about that. My wife gets all the mail, and she isn't here right now," he said as he tried to close the door.

Mercedes stopped the door with her hand.

"If you could be a dear and answer a few questions it would really help me out. I've still got a hundred houses to interview tonight. Mercy me! My feet are killing me."

"Okay sure," said the man. "But make it quick. My game show is almost on."

Mercedes asked questions super fast. "So just you and your wife live here. Any children?"

"Uh, no."

"Any dogs?"

"What?" he asked confused by her question.

"I asked if there are any dogs living in this house. The city needs this information. We track all humans and dogs now."

"Oh, sure. My wife has a dog… and a bird."

"We don't care about birds. May I see the dog please?" asked Mercedes.

"I actually hate the dog. If there's a problem with the paperwork, you can take the dog with you."

The man whistled and a tan yipping Chihuahua came running up to the door.

"Uh no, this one definitely won't work," said Mercedes in her normal voice. There was no way she could trick Austen to thinking this was his dog.

"Do you wanna take it?" the man asked.

"Please!"

Mercedes changed her voice back to a southern accent, "No, no. I have everything I need here. The city thanks you," Mercedes said as she ran away.

Evangeline watched her sisters run from door to door. Neither of them were finding new suspects. Giselle was asked several times if she was a babysitter. One lady even handed her a crying baby while she looked at the flyer.

Mercedes played a different character at every door, and each character lied with a different accent. One man believed her lie about working for a lawn company that sprays for weeds. He even gave her $20.

Time passed, and Evangeline grew bored watching her sisters strike out. She decided to do some detective work of her own. "Like I told them, to find a dog you have to think like a dog," she said.

Still wearing her dog costume Evangeline walked into a neighbor's messy yard on all fours. She sniffed the grass looking for clues. This front yard was full of smelly stained sofas, run down refrigerators, and old junky cars with flat tires. A chubby man in his 30's with a scruffy beard ran out of the garage.

"Hey there! These are my treasures and they ain't for sale," he said.

Evangeline was confused at what he could possibly be calling his "treasures." She perked up her dog ears and listened carefully for any dog barks. There was nothing. This guy was clean. And by "clean" she meant he wasn't guilty.

"Scram! Get out of here!" the man shouted. "You weird dog girl."

Evangeline lifted her leg. She pretended to pee on the junky car sitting in the driveway. That's what dogs did when they wanted to be rude. "Ruff ruff," Evangeline barked and quickly scampered away.

Giselle, back on her side of the street, was upset because she had fallen behind. It seemed like every conversation she had with the homeowners took twice as long as Mercedes. She was determined to get done with this next house as quickly as possible.

Giselle noticed a strange woman looking at her through the curtain. The woman ducked down when Giselle made eye contact with her. On the porch Giselle spotted a lot of white animal fur all over the rocking chair.

"Bingo has white hair," she muttered to

herself. Giselle knocked on the door. No answer. She knocked again. Nothing.

"Umm. Hello," Giselle said nervously. "I know you're inside. I saw you. Can I ask you a few questions about your dog?"

"I don't have a dog!" yelled the strange woman. Again the woman peeked through the curtain. This time Giselle noticed she was holding a large animal with white fur.

Giselle couldn't just call the woman a liar. Even though she was.

"Please leave. You're making me uncomfortable," the woman begged.

"I'm sorry, but I really need to know about your dog," pleaded Giselle. "The animals in this neighborhood might be in serious danger."

The word danger instantly got the woman's attention. She opened the front door. An army of fluffy cats came running out.

"My cats are in danger? What kind of danger?" she asked worriedly.

There were more cats than Giselle could count. "Not cats ma'am. Only dogs."

"I told you I don't have a dog," the woman responded annoyed.

"But I saw a white dog in your window," Giselle exclaimed.

"Chester. Here!" she called.

A very large white cat waddled through the front door. He let out a long grouchy meow. The woman continued to talk to the cat, "See this is why you need to go on a diet. People think you're a dog. Okay family. Who thinks Chester should go on a diet?"

The cats all meowed. Chester hissed back. Giselle quickly said goodbye to the crazy cat lady and ran out of there.

Mercedes watched Giselle run to the next house. Mercedes was still a few houses in the lead, but she was feeling certain that she would win. Sure she didn't have any suspects, but she didn't care as long as she won the bet.

"Looks like you're having trouble keeping up," Mercedes shouted to Giselle.

"It's not over yet," Giselle yelled back as she ran faster.

Mercedes bolted up to her next house. She pounded on the door. The woman who answered could see Mercedes was in a panic.

"Help! Please!" begged Mercedes pretending to be out of breath. "There's a dog on the loose. He's a grey and white husky. I've been told he may have rabies. We need to find him right away!"

"Oh my!" said the woman concerned. "I haven't seen any loose dogs."

"Do you have a dog? He could be at risk for rabies!" shouted Mercedes.

"No," the woman answered worriedly.

Mercedes handed the woman Bingo's flyer. "Please if you see or hear anything call the number on this flyer immediately!" She ran off to the sidewalk, slowing down before getting to the next house. "It's sad that no one gets to see my amazing performances today," she said to herself.

Evangeline decided to stop and admire a sprinkler. She watched as it watered the front yard. She stuck out her tongue to get a quick drink. When she turned to leave she was surrounded by a group of toddlers. She looked around, but didn't see any parents.

"Hi puppy!" yelled a cute little two-year-old girl.

Evangeline looked at the kids' smiles and decided to have some fun. She rolled over. She played dead. She even put her mouth on the gross looking stick that one of them wanted her to play fetch with. The kids took turns petting her and playing with her dog ears.

"Arf! Arf!" barked Evangeline. *Okay. Time to*

go, she decided.

She tried to back away but the toddlers didn't let go.

"Puppy no bye bye," a little boy yelled.

They all grabbed her and held on tight. They piled on top of her. These kids weren't cute, they were monsters! Evangeline had to escape. But how? She let out her loudest dog bark.

"RRRRRRRUUUFFFFF!!!" she barked. She growled as she showed her teeth!

The toddlers were shocked. They let go long enough for Evangeline to grab a stick.

"Fetch!" she yelled as she threw it.

The kids all ran after the stick. Then Evangeline got out of there lickety split. She ran and ran on two legs until finally she caught up with her sisters down the street.

"What's wrong?" asked Giselle.

"Out of breath," Evangeline answered, "Toddlers... Death grip... Almost died."

"Where are our backpacks?" said Giselle more worried about her bag than Evangeline's drama.

Evangeline pointed back down the street, "In the bushes by the house with all the treasure out front," she answered.

Giselle rolled her eyes, "Great. One more

thing for me to deal with. You better hope no one steals them. Just stay with me and don't wander off."

At that moment it started to drizzle. Seconds later it was pouring down rain. Then a piercing scream filled the air. Someone was in trouble.

"Mercedes!" Giselle realized and took off running. Evangeline followed on two legs but couldn't keep up. Giselle ran faster than she had ever run in her life. Something was wrong. She just hoped that she could get there in time.

Out of breath and unable to talk, Giselle arrived at the house where Mercedes was standing under a tree.

"This fabric is dry clean only!" Mercedes wailed.

"I thought you were hurt. Or kidnapped!" Giselle said angrily.

"This is much worse!" cried Mercedes.

"That's it. Bet's off. We're going home," ordered Giselle.

The girls grabbed their backpacks Evangeline had hidden. They held the bags like umbrellas over their heads as they slowly walked back to the bus stop. Cold, wet, and hungry, they sat in silence as they rode the bus home.

The sisters had nothing to show for their day of work. They had no clues, no new leads, and no suspects. Worst of all, with Bingo still missing, they had no hope.

CHAPTER 7

The sisters walked into their house wet, tired, and feeling defeated. Luckily they got home before Mom and Dad. They decided they had better clean themselves up before their parents saw them and started asking questions.

"I call the first shower!" shouted Mercedes as she dropped her backpack and ran down the hall.

"Hurry up!" yelled Giselle. She turned to Evangeline to help her take off the dog collar. "You know she's going to take forever in there."

"Yup," said Evangeline. She unzipped and removed her dog costume. "I kinda don't want to take this off. It's fun being a dog."

"You were a great dog today," said Giselle with a smile. "Now put this collar back in Dad's camera bag before they get home. I'm going to go hurry Mercedes out of the shower."

Evangeline stopped by the kitchen on the way to her parents' office. She was still hungry and decided she'd better get a snack before Mom got home. Who knew what gross dinner she would cook up tonight. There was a box of fruit snacks hidden on a shelf. "Score!" But when she picked up the snacks behind the box there were several cans of bacon dog treats.

Evangeline couldn't believe her luck. She reached for them, but her arms weren't long enough. This gave her an idea.

She used the dog collar like a rope to pull the can from the back of the shelf. Right when the can reached the edge, it fell to the ground and so did the collar. CRACK! The collar camera broke open and the small battery rolled under the fridge.

"Oh no!" thought Evangeline.

Just then her parents' car pulled into the driveway. She had to act fast. She grabbed the can of treats and a package of fruit snacks for dessert. She ran down the hall to her parents' office. She kept trying to close the battery door on the camera, but no luck. Quickly she licked a fruit snack and stuck it inside the battery door.

"Perfect!" she said as the battery door clicked shut. Now the camera didn't look broken. Her plan didn't include what to do when Dad found out. She would worry about that later.

"Girls!" shouted Mom from the kitchen. "We got pizza."

Evangeline dashed to the kitchen upon hearing the magical word "pizza."

"Hey kiddo," said Dad as he gave Evangeline a hug. "Where are your sisters?"

Evangeline shrugged her shoulders. Her tummy was on a mission. It needed pizza.

Mom opened the box. The smell of cheesy goodness filled the air. Evangeline's face turned into a frown when all of the sudden she smelled onions.

"I got extra veggies so it's more healthy," said Mom as she gave Evangeline a slice. "Whoa! You need a bath! Why are you so dirty?"

"I was a dog today," said Evangeline as she picked the onions off her pizza. "I made lots of new dog friends. Can I have them over to play sometime?"

"Maybe," Mom said holding her nose. "We'll talk about that later. Dad and I have to get back to work so make sure your sisters get some pizza, okay?" Mom leaned down and gave Evangeline a kiss on the cheek. "But seriously, get a bath before bed."

Mom and Dad discussed what work they still needed to finish as they walked down the hall. Evangeline popped open a can of bacon treats and sprinkled them on her pizza. She gobbled down the slice then carried the pizza box to the bedroom she and Mercedes shared.

Their bedroom was a mix of colors and styles. On one side all of the decorations were only pink and black. Mercedes' two favorite colors. Evangeline's side of the room looked like a rainbow had exploded. There were bright colors everywhere.

Mercedes kept her side of the room neat and tidy. Evangeline's side was more like a disaster zone. When Evangeline set the pizza box down on her side of the room, you could barely see it in the mess.

"Mom got pizza," said Evangeline.

Mercedes turned from the mirror where she was counting brush strokes. "Forty-six, forty-seven, forty-eight," she counted as she brushed her wet hair. "Good pizza or Mom pizza? Forty-nine, fifty."

"Mom pizza," responded Evangeline.

Giselle entered the room wearing a towel on her head. "I smell pizza."

"Don't get excited," Mercedes said as she put her brush neatly away in her dresser. "It's Mom pizza."

Evangeline opened the box. The girls all groaned at the sight of veggies piled higher than the cheese. They each grabbed a slice and sat on the floor. The sisters picked off the vegetables and threw them back in the box as they discussed what they were going to do next.

"I've got to finish my spy report," explained Giselle as she licked tomato sauce off her fingers. "Did you bring any napkins?"

Evangeline dug around her messy floor. She found an old dirty napkin and handed it to Giselle. "Guys we can't give up on Bingo now," begged Evangeline. "He needs us."

"No. We looked all day!" whined Mercedes. "We got rained on and chased by dogs and we almost died! Plus that stupid black dog shampoo won't come off my hand! $500 is not enough for all this drama."

"I agree," said Giselle. "I don't think being detectives is our thing."

"Let's just stick to making videos," said Mercedes as she flicked a mushroom off her pizza. The mushroom landed on the towel on Giselle's head, but Mercedes didn't tell her.

"Poor Austen," Giselle said with a sigh. "He's such a good guy. He doesn't deserve to lose his best friend. Let's face it, Mom and Dad are going to pick a different dog for the commercial whether we find Bingo or not."

"But Bingo needs us! We can't give up," pleaded Evangeline. "GEM Sisters are supposed to work together. Like Dad told us. Remember?"

"Sorry sis. Not this time," Giselle said, not knowing there was still a mushroom on her head. She stood to leave. "School comes first."

"Do we have any cucumbers?" asked Mercedes as she walked out of the room. "My eyes are so puffy from this super stressful day."

Evangeline watched her sisters leave the room. She looked down at the pizza box now filled with pizza crusts and vegetables.

Evangeline looked over to her backpack and saw Bingo's flyer sticking out of the side zipper. She stared at his picture sadly. She took one last look at his fluffy white fur and big cute blue eyes. She let out a deep sigh.

"Sorry Bingo," she said. She crumpled the paper and threw it on her pile of junk.

After taking a bath, Evangeline wandered into the living room. She hoped that watching some television would distract her from feeling so sad. She dug in the couch cushions looking for the remote.

"Stop it!" ordered Mercedes laying on the couch. "I was here first. My skin needs quiet!" On her face was a green mud mask, with sliced cucumbers on her eyes. Mercedes believed a girl could never start too early when it came to preventing wrinkles. She repeated one of her favorite chants.

"You are Mercedes... the most beautiful of the three. Like a star you'll shine... for all the world to see."

Evangeline felt too gloomy to fight back. Instead, she found the remote, turned on the TV, and plopped down on the couch. A cartoon dog raced across the screen chasing a cartoon cat.

"Seriously?" she groaned. "For one second I'd like to not think about dogs." She popped open another can of dog treats and dumped the whole can into her mouth.

The bacon smell went straight to Mercedes' nose, "Gross! Haven't you already eaten like two cans today?"

"I don't keep track anymore," mumbled Evangeline with her mouth full.

Just then Mom and Dad entered the room. Their hands overflowed with pictures of dogs. These were special pictures called headshots. On the front was a picture of the dog and on the back was a typed list of all the special tricks the dog could do.

"Girls we need your opinion," said Dad holding up a picture of a golden retriever.

Great, more dogs, Evangeline thought to herself annoyed.

"Giselle get in here," Mom called out.

Mom and Dad loved to work together, but they didn't always agree on what they should do. The girls were used to listening to them argue about their work, but their parents called it "discussing."

Giselle entered the room holding her essay on a clipboard. "I really need to finish this. I can't get a bad grade and ruin my chance of getting into a good college."

"This will only take a second," Mom promised.

Giselle pushed Mercedes' feet off the couch and sat down.

"Do you know what all of this stress is doing to my skin?" Mercedes said as she pulled the cucumbers off her eyes. "I haven't posted a video in days and look, I'm getting a zit!" She pointed to a very small bump on her chin. No one tried to look.

"Let's talk about your girl problems after we're done," said Dad instantly wishing he hadn't opened his mouth. Being the only boy in the family meant he was always outnumbered and usually forced to talk about things that made him feel uncomfortable.

"Girls we can't decide who to cast in the commercial," explained Mom.

"I vote ME!" shouted Mercedes waving her hand in the air.

"No!" Mom and Dad both said in unison.

"You see, Dad wants to choose a dog that looks boring and can't do anything special," said Mom in a joking tone.

"And Mom wants a dog that is going to scare everyone because it looks like a bank robber wearing a mask," responded Dad. He grabbed an empty can of bacon treats and held it like a gun. "Give me all your bacon or else I'm going to poop in your yard!"

The girls all let out a giggle.

"Why is that funny?" asked Mom.

"He said poop," Evangeline explained then giggled again. "Poop makes people laugh. You should put poop in your commercial."

Dad tossed Mom the can of bacon treats. He smiled as if he had already won. Mom shook the can. She popped off the lid and looked inside. "Why is this can empty?" she asked.

Giselle, Mercedes, and Dad all looked to Evangeline. She quickly spoke to change the subject, "You should let us choose the dog for the commercial."

"Agreed!" said Dad. He decided it was better to possibly lose to Mom than to have her find out that he let Evangeline eat dog treats.

Mom could tell something was fishy, but she cared more about her dog winning. Mom liked to win at everything. "Fine. You go first dear."

"Girls I just ask that you choose the dog you think the audience will love most." He held up a picture of the dog of his choice. "This is Sir-Barks-A-Lot."

"Awwww," said the girls in unison.

"More like Sir-Stinks-A-Lot," muttered Mom.

Dad ignored Mom and addressed the girls, "I present to you America's favorite dog. A golden retriever." Dad opened his laptop and pressed play.

A video audition played. Sir-Barks-A-Lot

walked on his two back feet. He hopped up and down. The girls "oohed" and "aahed." Their faces lit up. Dad was feeling very good about his dog choice. He could tell Mom was getting nervous.

On screen for his ending trick, Sir Barks-A-Lot picked up a ball with his mouth and tossed it high in the air. The ball landed in the bucket next to the dog and he let out a bark. Dad stopped the video and explained his idea for the commercial.

"See, Sir Barksy, that's what I call him, will pick up the bacon treat and toss it into the air. It will then fall perfectly into the dog food bowl. What do you think?" said Dad.

The girls clapped and cheered. "Ha! In your face!" teased Dad to Mom.

"It's not over yet," she teased back. "Girls, I can totally understand why you'd want to pick Sir-Stinks, I mean Sir-Barks-A-Lot. But keep in mind, I can make different spinach meals every night this week OR we could go out to the restaurant of your choice. It's up to you."

"Hey! That is so not fair," said Dad. "You can't threaten the voters."

"We didn't agree to any rules. And who said I play fair?" asked Mom with a sneaky smile.

Dad folded his arms and shook his head no.

"Fine," groaned Mom. "Girls I now present to you. The cute, the cuddly, the super talented puppy, TACO!'

Mom held up a picture of an adorable black husky puppy with bright blue eyes. Dad was right, the little mask of white fur around his eyes did make him look like a robber. But in an adorable stuffed animal kind of way.

"He's so cute!" squealed Evangeline. "You just want to hug him!"

Dad mumbled, "What kind of name is Taco? Sounds like lunch, not a dog star."

Mom handed the picture to Giselle then pushed play on Taco's audition video on the laptop. Taco popped onto the screen. First, he got up on his legs and walked backwards with a smile.

"A smile?" Dad thought to himself, "How do you teach a dog how to smile?"

"I forget. Could your dog smile?" asked Mom with a smirk.

"No talking!" ordered Dad.

Taco jumped through a hoop and then hopped on a skateboard. His cute little black paws peddled on the ground.

"Now picture this," Mom said excitedly.

"Taco skates across the screen. He sees a bacon treat on the counter. Oh no! How can he get the treat off the counter? He jumps through a hoop high in the air catching the bacon treat in his mouth. Then he's so proud of himself, what does he do?"

Mom pointed to the screen where Taco performed his final trick. Not just one, but TWO BACK FLIPS!

The girls all jumped up and cheered in unison, "BINGO!"

Mom beamed with pride, "That's right! You heard the girls. Bingo! My dog wins!" she said as she did a silly victory dance.

"Alright. Don't rub it in. You win this time," said Dad as he followed Mom dancing down the hall to the office.

Evangeline ran off to her room and was back in a flash holding the flyer. She held it up to the picture Giselle had of Taco. On the flyer she scribbled black pen across Bingo's face, making him look like the dog in the picture.

"Look at the eyes!" Mercedes said excitedly. "They're exactly the same!"

"Bingo is the only dog who can do two back flips in a row," Evangeline reminded her sisters.

Giselle looked closely at both pictures. "That

means either this dog Taco is the second dog we
know who can do that trick… or Taco IS Bingo."

CHAPTER 8

The next day craziness filled the house. Filming days were always like this. No matter how much time they had to prepare, Mom and Dad were always rushing to get out the door. Mom ran around eating a healthy bowl of cereal as she gathered important paperwork to throw in her purse. As she set down the bowl, milk spilled all over her papers. "Not today," she groaned grabbing a napkin.

The girls hid out in Giselle's room so their parents would think they were still asleep. Evangeline spied through the window and watched Dad quickly run in and out of the house. He was frantically grabbing gear he needed to film the commercial. All of his filming stuff in the van left only room in the two front seats.

"We're good to go," Evangeline explained to

her sisters. "No empty seats in the van. They definitely can't bring us to the film set."

"Perfect," said Giselle. "Operation boyfriend is a go!"

Mercedes looked at Giselle with a confused face. "Operation boyfriend?"

Giselle tried to cover her words, "I said Bingo. Operation Bingo is a go."

Mercedes spoke in a deep boy voice, "Hey. Wanna be my girlfriend or whatever?" Then she squealed in high girl voice, "Oh Austen, I love you! Yes!" Mercedes wrapped her arms around herself and made loud kissy noises.

Giselle groaned and left the room. Even though Mercedes was making fun of her she secretly hoped it would come true. She smiled and sighed at the thought of her first kiss.

Evangeline's tummy growled. "I hear you! We had to wait until it was clear. Now we can go. Geesh you're so bossy!" She walked out of the room and down to the kitchen.

The girls all searched for breakfast options in the pantry. Meanwhile, Mom and Dad raced around the house, trying to leave. Evangeline opened an empty cabinet. Mom had clearly been too busy working to get groceries. She unhappily grabbed the box of healthy cereal.

"Where's my lucky underwear?" yelled Dad as he carried a big light.

"I haven't seen 'em," shouted Mom as she held up a hair dryer to the wet papers trying to blow them dry. "I've got my own problems. The film permits are wet."

Dad dashed back into the kitchen. "Honey, I can't film without my lucky underwear," he whined.

Mercedes muttered to her sisters, "We'd all be a whole lot luckier if he washed them once in awhile."

Mom complained as she followed Dad out of the kitchen to help him look. As soon as their parents left the room, the girls dashed into action. Giselle went to the hall to act as a lookout while Evangeline and Mercedes searched through Mom's pile of sticky papers.

"Found it!" said Evangeline. She held up the headshot with Taco the dog's face.

Mercedes used her phone to take a picture. Then she flipped over the paper and took a picture of the information typed on the back.

"What time is Taco supposed to be on set?" asked Mercedes.

Evangeline flipped through the pile of papers. She found one titled "call sheet" that had a list of times for the day. "He's supposed to arrive at twelve-o-clock," read Evangeline.

"That only gives us four hours to find him!" Mercedes said. She was about to take a picture of the call sheet when she heard Giselle sneeze. That was their signal.

Giselle sneezed again when she saw her parents rushing down the hall toward her. "Oh hey Dad!" she yelled. "Did you find your lucky underwear? I was just going to come and help you look!" Giselle spoke loudly hoping her sisters heard her.

"Got 'em on!" he said as he bolted through the kitchen.

Giselle entered to see her sisters at the table eating bowls of cereal. Evangeline quickly flashed Giselle a thumbs up. She was having fun being sneaky and working together as a team.

Mom shoved the papers from the counter into her purse. "Girls we don't have any room to take you with us so what are you doing today?" she said.

"Don't worry Mom. We were just planning on staying home and filming some videos," answered Giselle.

Mercedes kicked Giselle from under the

table. "Ow!" squealed Giselle as she glared back at her.

"Or we might go to the park," added Mercedes. "I've been needing to take some new pictures and you know how great my skin looks in natural light. I was thinking maybe we could do a GEM Sisters' photo shoot. But seriously Mom, I really need to talk to you about getting some new clothes and-"

Just as she planned, Mom interrupted her.

"Sounds good. Giselle, you're in charge. If you go out, be safe and don't talk to strangers. We should be back after dinner. Here's some money so you can order food, but eat something healthy!" Mom ran to the table and gave each sister a kiss on the head. "Love you. I'm late. I've got my phone if you need me!" she said as she ran out the front door.

The girls watched out the window as Mom ran to the van juggling her purse, papers, water bottle, and a bagel piled high with cream cheese for Dad. He was already in the driver's seat, buckled in. Dad reached across and pushed open the passenger door for Mom since her hands were full. She shoved the bagel in his face and he took a giant bite as she buckled her seatbelt.

Dad threw the car in gear and sped off, neither one of them seeing that Dad had a cream cheese moustache. The girls turned away from the window when they knew the coast was clear.

"Why did you kick me?" Giselle asked Mercedes.

"Because your lie would have gotten us in trouble," Mercedes explained. "You said we were going to stay home, but my lie got us permission to leave the house. That way, if we get caught later, we can act like Mom said yes."

"Giselle, learn from the master," Evangeline said, bowing to Mercedes.

"And," added Mercedes, "Mom said don't talk to strangers, but she didn't say we couldn't track them down."

Together, the girls looked at Mercedes' phone where she had taken photos of Mom's papers. First, they studied the photo of Taco and compared it to the picture of Bingo on Austen's flyer. Then they viewed the next picture with all of the dog's typed information.

"Who is Joseph Miller?" asked Evangeline pointing to the phone.

"It's the name of the dog's owner," Giselle explained.

"More like the guy who stole him. Let's see what he looks like," Mercedes said as she typed his name into a search website on her phone. "One million results! How are we ever going to find him in time?"

The sisters knew they needed to prove that Taco was a stolen dog before their parents started filming their commercial, and time was running out.

"Let's say we find the dog. Even if we can prove that he's Bingo, how are we going to explain it to Mom and Dad?" questioned Mercedes.

"We will figure it out together," said Giselle. "But first we need to find out if we're right about Taco and Bingo being the same dog." Giselle pointed to the address listed by Joseph Miller's name. Then she noticed the clock by the oven. "The next bus leaves in fifteen minutes. We gotta hurry!"

Giselle and Evangeline bolted from the table to get ready to go. Mercedes sat there stunned. "You're kidding, right? I need more than fifteen minutes to get ready."

"Now it's fourteen minutes!" shouted Giselle from her bedroom.

Mercedes was up in a flash. Fourteen

minutes later, the sisters were getting on a crowded bus.

After a bumpy bus ride, the three girls found themselves walking in a neighborhood they knew their parents would not approve of. There were abandoned shopping carts, trash-filled alleys, and lots of chewed up gum stuck on the sidewalk.

"Definitely won't be trying any gum from here," Evangeline said with regret as she stepped over an extra gooey pink blob.

Giselle compared the address on the dog's headshot with the numbers on the upcoming apartment buildings. They were getting closer. As they walked, the girls tried to figure out who Joseph Miller could be.

"Maybe he's partners with Harold Farnblatt," explained Mercedes. "I picture this is the kind of gross place he would live. And together they kidnap famous dogs."

Giselle nodded yes at the possibility. Mercedes' theory made a lot of sense, but she had her own idea. "Maybe that mean fish lady neighbor kidnapped Bingo and then sold him. Joseph could have bought the dog not knowing he was stolen."

"Well whoever took the dog clearly did it

for the money. I mean I would totally steal if it meant getting out of this neighborhood. Ew!" Mercedes said stepping over a giant pile of trash.

"What if we're thinking about this all wrong?" Evangeline wondered out loud. "What if Joseph isn't a person at all? What if Bingo was kidnapped by another dog? Think about it. There could be a dog boss who kidnaps dogs and forces them into show business. He keeps all the money and then when the puppies grow up and lose their cuteness, he forces them to live a life of crime stealing the next cute batch of puppies!"

Her sisters politely said nothing to Evangeline's weird thoughts.

Evangeline continued, "It's true that I haven't found a dog that can speak human yet. But that doesn't mean they can't. The dogs are probably hiding their advanced skills to protect their criminal operation."

Giselle decided to ignore her crazy theory and keep walking. "Well this is the right address, but it doesn't say which apartment number," said Giselle as she pointed to a huge building.

A sign on the front door read:

RESIDENTS ONLY.

To the left side of the door was a list of residents' names next to their individual apartment number. There were fifty apartments in the building. The names were each typed on a sticky label and stuck on the list next to their number.

"I don't see Joseph Miller," whined Mercedes. She started looking again at the top of the list.

Evangeline pointed out that several of the name labels were missing. "Maybe he moved?"

Giselle looked down and saw a pile of trash by the door. "Argh!" she shouted.

Frustrated, she kicked the trash with her foot. That's when she noticed a few name labels in the pile. "They must have peeled off in the hot sun!" she said excitedly.

Giselle read the names aloud until she found the one she was looking for. "J. Miller! Number 204."

"Let's go get this dirtbag!" said Mercedes as she pulled on the handle. The door didn't move because it was locked. "Why would they lock the door?"

"To stop people like us from sneaking in," explained Giselle.

The girls waited for someone who lived in the building to go in, but for an hour no one came or went. They needed to get inside and they were running out of time.

"Maybe we could climb up from the outside?" said Evangeline as she studied the front of the building, looking for open windows. She set her backpack down on the sidewalk and dug around inside. "What was I thinking? Why did I pack all of these stuffed animals instead of rope?"

"I'm bored," complained Mercedes. "And hot. Evangeline, did you bring any water?"

Evangeline looked in her backpack. She shook her head no. "But I brought my library card. We can go there later. They have my favorite water fountain. It's ice cold."

"Great idea!" said Mercedes. She grabbed the library card and stuck it into the door. "I saw this in a movie. They used a credit card and wiggled it around and then 'click' the door unlocked."

CRACK! The card snapped in half. "Evangeline do you have any other cards?" Mercedes asked as she handed back the broken card.

"Seriously! This is why Mom doesn't trust you to get your own library card," said

Evangeline as she tossed it back in her bag.

"Maybe Joseph already left?" said Giselle. "It's almost noon. He probably wanted to get an early start so he could avoid traffic."

Giselle and Mercedes discussed what to do next. Evangeline hadn't let go of her plan to climb up from the outside. Maybe she could get on top of a car parked on the street and jump to the closest window.

Evangeline spotted a white van in the row of cars. *That's even higher than a car so it should totally work,* she thought to herself. She looked for the best place to climb up and then she saw it. The side of the van read:

PAWS AND CLAWS GROOMING.

A loud whistle filled the air. Giselle and Mercedes turned to see it came from Evangeline pointing to the van she had discovered. They rushed over.

"This is Jack's van," realized Giselle.

"Maybe he's inside washing a dog," said Evangeline. She banged on the van door before her sisters could stop her.

When Jack didn't answer the girls peeked inside the van windows. There was no one.

Giselle wondered, "Jack wouldn't take Bingo... would he?"

"No. Jack can't be the pup-napper because he's really nice. And the bad guy's name is Joseph," said Evangeline relieved.

Mercedes pulled a bobby pin out of her hair, "There's only one way to find out." She put the bobby pin into the keyhole trying to unlock the back door. She wiggled the pin around but no luck. The pin just got bent. "Hmm. This always works on Giselle's diary."

Before Giselle could get angry, Evangeline walked up and pressed the secret button to open the two back doors. She remembered Jack using it before. CLICK! The doors opened.

Going inside the van was wrong, but Giselle knew she couldn't turn back now. For the first time she felt like the answers were right in front of her. She took charge, "Mercedes, you and I are going in. Evangeline, you stand guard. Let us know if anyone comes near. We are getting to the bottom of this mystery right now."

Evangeline pouted as she watched her sisters get in the van, "What? Stand guard? But I'm the one who found the van." Annoyed, she sat down on the sidewalk and looked for a snack in her backpack.

Inside the van, Giselle and Mercedes looked

for clues. "Look at this mess," explained Giselle. She sorted through different drawers of dog brushes, bows and nail clippers.

"It smells even worse than it looks," said Mercedes holding her nose. "I thought Evangeline was messy."

Outside they could hear Evangeline complaining. "What's going on in there? Did you find anything? It's boring out here!"

"Quiet down! And keep on the lookout!" Giselle said in a loud whisper. She turned to Mercedes. "Hurry and look for clues," Giselle ordered as she scanned the van. She looked for anything that could help them find Bingo.

"Is this a clue?" asked Mercedes, holding up a leash.

"No," said Giselle annoyed.

"Is this a clue?" asked Mercedes, picking up a gum wrapper.

"No, said Giselle.

"Is this-" started Mercedes.

"NO!" Giselle interrupted. "NOT everything is a clue. Now come on. If Jack did take Bingo then we need proof. Hurry up!"

Mercedes found a drawer of brushes and got distracted again. She ran her fingers through a big white brush. Was it horsehair she wondered? How could the bristles be so stiff yet still feel so gentle?

Mercedes began brushing her hair with the dog brush. "Hmm, feels good on my scalp." She sighed and wondered, "When am I going to get my own salon trailer?"

"What are you doing?" Giselle hissed.

Suddenly there was a whisper that sounded very close. "Did you guys find any bacon treats in here?"

Giselle jumped! It was Evangeline standing right next to her. "What are you doing? You're supposed to be on watch!" said Giselle. "Get back to your post!"

Right as she finished her words, the back doors closed. She saw that Mercedes had shut them.

Giselle couldn't hide her anger, "Why did you do that?"

"Because someone is coming out of the apartment and I didn't want them to see us," said Mercedes proud of herself.

In a panic, Giselle looked out the window. Jack was carrying a dog crate and heading straight for the van. "Oh my gosh! Oh my gosh! Oh my gosh! Girls, hide!"

Quickly Evangeline scooted into the dog

grooming chair and faced it to the wall to remain hidden. Mercedes closed herself inside a small closet by the counter and pinched her nose to avoid the smell. There were no more good places to hide, so Giselle jumped in the dirty dog tub and covered herself in a pile of wet stinky dog towels.

They stayed quiet for what seemed like forever. Giselle thought the coast was clear. But just as she poked her head up, the front passenger door opened. She watched as Jack buckled up the crate with a black husky puppy inside.

Giselle's mind was racing. Jack was walking to the front of the van. She knew there was no way they could all get out quick enough. Before she could think of anything, the van was moving. There was nothing she could do to help her sisters now. They were trapped!

CHAPTER 9

The girls held on tight as Jack sped through town. He was clearly in a hurry, which helped the girls remain hidden in the back of the van. Jack steered the clunky old van into a turn, way too fast. The tires squealed. Bottles and brushes rolled around like bowling pins in the back of the van. The noise from the loud old engine covered the sounds of the girls' whispers.

Giselle looked through a small eyehole she had formed with the gross wet towels on her head. "Don't worry," Giselle said softly. "Everything is going to be fine."

"Where are we going?" asked Mercedes.

"I don't know," Giselle answered, trying to hide her panic.

"Do you see any bacon treats?" whispered Evangeline. Yes, she knew what was happening was serious, but so was the growl in her tummy. If she didn't get a snack soon, her loud stomach might give them away.

Jack's phone rang. He pushed the button to answer, "Paws and Claws Grooming. We take care of everything."

"More like take your dog," Mercedes said annoyed.

Giselle shushed Mercedes. So far Jack didn't know they were back there and she wanted to keep it that way.

"I am on set for the rest of day working on a commercial, but I can come over first thing tomorrow for a wash and style," Jack said into the phone. He politely said goodbye and hung up.

Thanks to the phone call, Giselle knew for sure where they were going. She started to whisper, but suddenly the van slowed down making the engine grow quiet. The van softly rumbled as it waited at a red light. Giselle made eye contact with Evangeline and motioned for her to be still. She looked over to Mercedes to do the same, but she was too busy looking at her phone to notice.

Mercedes still had plans to make a video of them finding the dog. She wasn't going to miss an opportunity to get a lot of views and become famous. Mercedes held up the phone to film Giselle hiding under the pile of smelly wet towels. She mouthed the words 'smile' to her sister.

In a panic, Giselle shook her head, causing the small towel on her face to fall off. The dog instantly turned in his cage and made eye contact with Giselle. She grabbed the towel in a flash, but her hand accidentally knocked over a bottle. BANG! The dog started barking!

Immediately Jack turned towards the back of the van. The dog barked louder. He was jumping and shaking in his cage. Jack looked at the mess in the back. He didn't notice Giselle who sat very still under the pile of towels. The small towel, back over her face, was slowly slipping. Any second, it would fall off and Jack would see her.

The dog's piercing barks came even faster and louder. Jack shouted, "Quiet! Stop barking! Shut up!" The dog ignored him and continued to bark. "You want a treat or something? Fine!"

Jack looked at the red light then put the van into park. He unbuckled his seatbelt and climbed in between the front seats to the back of the van. The girls' eyes grew wider as he got closer and closer to Giselle.

With a towel over her face, Giselle couldn't see what was happening, but she could hear Jack moving things around her. Giselle held her breath so her body wouldn't move.

"Where are those treats at?" Jack asked himself. He picked a brush off the ground and threw it into the tub.

Mercedes watched in horror as Jack crept closer to Giselle. She wanted to help, but she couldn't think of what to do. Jack's hand reached in the tub and lifted a towel uncovering Giselle's shoe. HONK! HONK! HONK!

Jack turned. The light was now green. Cars behind him were honking for him to move. He quickly ran to the front and jumped in his seat. "You're just gonna have to wait. They'll have plenty of treats for you when we get there."

Jack pressed hard on the gas pedal. The van rumbled loudly as it sped off. The dog continued to bark at the top of his lungs. Luckily all of the noise allowed the girls to take a breath of relief.

A few minutes later, the tires squealed and the van swerved into a parking spot. Jack's phone rang as he turned off the engine. He looked at the number on the screen then he cleared his throat and answered, "Hello. I just got here."

The girls recognized the muffled voice on the other end of the call. It was their mom. Her voice sounded like she was very annoyed.

"I'm so sorry I'm late. I was having trouble with my van starting, but I'm here now," Jack said as he opened the door. He walked around to the other side and opened the passenger door. "Yes, he's all groomed and ready just like you asked. Be right there."

Jack hung up the phone before saying goodbye. Quickly he grabbed the cage with the dog inside and slammed the door shut.

The girls waited for a second to make sure it was safe. Slowly, they crept out of their hiding places.

"If he's going to lie to Mom, he'd better practice some more," said Mercedes.

"That's what you learned from this?" Giselle asked annoyed. "What we just did was so wrong and really dangerous. Imagine what would have happened if we had been caught?"

Evangeline didn't have time to listen to her sisters argue. She threw on her backpack and popped open the back door. She instantly recognized where they were. It was the same building where their parents held the dog auditions.

Giselle grabbed the van door and pulled it shut before Evangeline could jump outside. "What are you doing?" scolded Giselle.

"I'm going to go tell Mom and Dad that I thought Jack was a good guy, but he's actually a criminal. And that we're pretty sure the dog he has with him is kidnapped. And that Mom is right, we should always wear seatbelts because riding in a car without them is really unsafe."

Hearing Evangeline tell the story, Giselle knew she was going to be in big, big, big trouble. Hopefully Austen would wait for her to be ungrounded in forty years.

Mercedes filmed a video of herself with her phone. "Guys I'm filming this from inside the bad guy's van. Great news! We didn't die and we caught the criminal. I'm pretty sure he's gonna go to jail for a long time. Side note! Look how good my hair still looks after hiding from the pup-napper in this creepy van."

Giselle gulped. Nope, forty years wasn't enough. She was going to be grounded for the rest of her life. "Mercedes! Turn off the camera now!" she shouted. "We're not going anywhere or telling anyone anything!"

"Why not? We're heroes!" Mercedes argued.

Giselle ignored her. She was busy working on a plan to get them home before Mom and Dad could find out what happened. She glanced at her phone. If they left now they could make the next bus and be home in an hour. They could still film a GEM Sisters' video and then Mom wouldn't ask any questions about their day.

"You can come or not, but I'm going to save Bingo," Evangeline said firmly.

"You can't go tell everyone that Jack's dog is Bingo. You don't have proof! I'm sorry. We failed. End of story. Let's go home and NOT get grounded."

"No. I'm staying," Evangeline said as she took off her backpack. "If we need proof then I'll find it."

Giselle watched as Evangeline dug through the pile of junk on the floor of the van.

"And I'm going to keep filming," said Mercedes kneeling down beside her. She knew she was close to getting that reward money. Now wasn't the time to quit.

Evangeline held up a brush and showed it to Mercedes. "Is this proof?"

"Maybe," Mercedes said shrugging her shoulders.

Next she held up a sparkly dog collar. "Is this proof?"

"Definitely," answered Mercedes as she wrapped the collar on her wrist like a bracelet.

Giselle groaned. She wanted to leave but she was stuck. Imagine if her parents found out she lost her two little sisters on top of everything else. "Fine. If we're going to find proof, then we need to know what kind of evidence we're looking for," she explained.

Mercedes and Evangeline struggled to pay attention as Giselle used her school essay about George Washington's spies to explain her point. To her sisters, it seemed like she rambled on forever, but in reality, it was only a few minutes.

Giselle wrapped up her explanation, "So that's why you can't simply blame someone and say they're guilty. To prove someone is a spy you would need to either catch them in the act or have whatever the spy stole as evidence. You have to show they're guilty."

"Okay, but we're not looking for stolen spy messages from the Revolutionary War," Mercedes responded annoyed. "Just tell us what we should look for."

Giselle tried to hide her smile. For once her

sisters had actually listened to her homework presentation. "We can't start with what we don't know, so let's start with what we do."

Evangeline raised her hand with excitement, "In your essay, you said the best way to solve a case was to go back to the beginning."

Giselle reached over and gave Evangeline a big hug. "Why are you hugging me?"

"Oh nothing. Never mind," Giselle said as she pulled back. She was definitely going to get an 'A' on her report if her little sisters liked it.

"Hello, bored over here," whined Mercedes reminding Giselle of the task at hand.

"Right. Okay. We know that Austen, who happens to have dreamy blue eyes, was planning to bring his dog Bingo to audition for the commercial. But the day before the audition, his dog went missing."

"He thought his dog ran away, so he looked everywhere and hung up flyers," added Evangeline. "And that's when we offered to help."

Mercedes excitedly joined the story. "And we thought the old weird guy Harold Farnblatt stole the dog because he wears super ugly clothes and has poorly dyed gross streaky hair."

Evangeline cleared her throat signaling

Mercedes to get to the facts.

Mercedes continued, "But you guys didn't care about his lack of fashion and were more focused on some mean comment he left on a video." Then she gasped, remembering what happened next. "But when we told Austen we were wrong about the pup-napping, he said we were right and showed us that strange note!"

"You mean this note?" said Evangeline as she pulled it out of her backpack.

"You kept the paper?" Mercedes asked. For the first time ever she was glad that her roommate was a packrat.

The sisters looked closely at the note, but nothing stood out as a clue.

"I don't want to rain on your parade, but I have to say it. What if we're wrong?" explained Giselle. "Jack is a dog groomer. Our parents could have hired him just to get the dog cleaned up for the commercial. Not to mention the dog's owners' name is Joseph, not Jack."

Mercedes opened the picture on her phone of the dog's headshot. She looked at the photo with the information typed on the back. Giselle had a very good point. Jack could have been at the apartment to pick up the dog after grooming him.

"Being a detective is so hard," complained Mercedes.

"Wait a second. Let me see that picture," Evangeline said as she grabbed the phone. "Look at this!" She held up the pup-napper's note to the phone. "Both of these are printed on the same color of light yellow paper."

Giselle looked at both the picture on the phone and the note to compare them. "Evangeline you're right!" She gave her a high five.

Mercedes held up her hand for a high five, but then pulled back when she noticed one of her nails was cracked. "Oh no!" She forgot to pack a nail file in her purse because Giselle rushed her out the door this morning. "Do you guys see a file in all this junk?"

"Now isn't the time to worry about your manicure," lectured Giselle. She continued to study the two papers looking for more clues.

Mercedes didn't agree. If she was going to be filmed as a hero today, she needed to look her best. She searched in the junk for a nail file. No luck. She climbed into the front of the van and searched in the glove box. Mercedes was hoping to find a personal grooming kit, but all she found were lots of random papers.

Giselle zoomed into the top right corner of the picture on the phone. Both it and the kidnapper's note had the same image with a rounded edge that had been torn. "Guys, what do you think was here? It's some sort of picture that was ripped off."

"It's a paw print," said Mercedes sure of herself. "Just like this one."

Mercedes handed Giselle a stack of light yellow papers. Each one had a black paw print on the top right-hand side of the page. The papers were a match.

"Great job Mercedes!" said Giselle as she held up her hand for a high five.

Mercedes smiled, proud of herself, and gave her sister a high five. She looked again at her broken nail but decided it would have to wait.

Evangeline noticed the name and address at the top of the paper Mercedes had found. She read it aloud, "Paws and Claws Grooming. Receipt For Services. Joseph Miller Owner." Excitedly she pointed to the image on the phone. "Look! The addresses are the same!"

The girls squealed with excitement.

Mercedes looked through the rest of the papers she had found. "Wow, this Joseph guy owes a lot of money on this hunk a junk van."

"I'm still confused. If this van belongs to this Joseph dude then why is Jack driving it around?" asked Evangeline.

Giselle had a feeling she knew why. On her phone, she typed the name "Joseph" into a search box for a website about baby names. She showed her sisters the results. "Just as I thought. Jack is a nickname for Joseph. They're the same person."

"Finally! We have proof. Can we leave this disgusting van now?" asked Mercedes.

"True, we have some proof, but only that he wrote the note to Austen. We still don't have proof that his dog Taco is actually Bingo," replied Giselle.

"You really think there could be two husky dogs that can do two back flips in a row?" asked Evangeline.

"Maybe," answered Giselle. "I'm saying it's possible and Austen just didn't know it."

The girls slumped in defeat. Mercedes looked at the time on her phone. It was 1:30, "Mom and Dad have already started filming," she informed her sisters.

"I demand justice!" yelled Evangeline. "We need to keep looking!"

The girls searched in the junk. "It's all so

gross," complained Mercedes. "How can he possibly get dogs clean in here? Everything you touch makes your hands dirty."

"That's it! Mercedes you're a genius!" Evangeline dug fast. She was throwing stuff everywhere.

"Watch it!" ordered Giselle as a shampoo bottle flew by her face. In that moment Giselle looked down at the black spot on the pup-napper's note and understood what Evangeline was looking for. "Mercedes you are a genius!" she agreed as she joined the search.

"I'm amazing. I get it. But why exactly?" Mercedes asked, confused.

Just then Evangeline found a bag full of garbage and emptied it into the pile of junk.

Giselle reached in and started sorting. She saw a banana peel, a giant ball of dog hair, and a box of moldy leftover half eaten rice. "Mercedes help us look!"

"Ew," whined Mercedes as she slowly reached her hand into the pile. "Could you at least tell me what we're looking for?"

"Found it!" yelled Evangeline. She held up a clear bottle filled with black slimy goo. "This is the bottle I grabbed the first time we met Jack. Mercedes remember? You said it was dog shampoo."

"Shampoo that dyes your hands. Look I finally got it to come off," she said holding up the palm of her hand. That's when she realized. "It's hair dye!"

"Exactly!" said Evangeline with a smile. "He's so busted!"

Mercedes was curious. "I didn't know you could dye dog's fur. I wonder how often you need to touch it up. I wanted to dye my hair blonde, but Mom said no because it cost too much to fix it as it grows out."

"And because you're too young to dye your hair," added Evangeline rolling her eyes.

"She might have said that too," Mercedes said not wanting to remember that part. "This is why Jack's hands were all gross. He didn't use gloves when he applied the dye!" For once Mercedes didn't mind the detective work since it involved beauty do's and don'ts.

"Of course!" shouted Giselle unable to hide her excitement. Giselle had found the dye kit box in the garbage pile. She read the list of ingredients on the back. "There's no ammonia or peroxide!"

"Pair-o-what?" questioned Evangeline. "Is that a type of dog treat? Because it sounds yummy."

Giselle tried to explain, "No. This dye doesn't use chemicals that make it long lasting. It doesn't attach to the hair like normal dye." She could tell by her sisters' blank faces that she wasn't doing a great job of explaining. "The dye rinses out!"

Mercedes gasped dramatically, "You're telling me that slimeball Jack dyed Bongo's fur black, but he used dye that's going to fade every time it gets wet? And that his fur will look terrible and streaky like Harold Farnblatt's hair? Now that's a crime!"

"All we have to do is get Bingo's fur wet and then the black dye will rinse out," said Giselle, proud of herself.

"Then let's go give him a bath!" shouted Evangeline.

Giselle and Mercedes turned to see Evangeline who was now wearing the dog costume.

"You had that in your backpack the whole day?" Mercedes asked.

"Nope. I never took it off. I thought it might come in handy and it's pretty comfortable under my clothes," said Evangeline. "Giselle, text Austen and tell him to get here quick. I've got the perfect plan to get Bingo back!"

CHAPTER 10

When the GEM Sisters entered the studio,
things were out of control. A film crew flew
around following Mom and Dad's orders. They
were taking care of last minute things. Dad
worked to get the lighting perfect on the bowl of
bacon treats. Mom was busy giving acting tips
to the actors including the dog.

"Wow! Look at the set," said Giselle. "Mom
and Dad really outdid themselves this time.
This commercial must be costing a lot of
money."

The sisters were impressed with the set
their parents had built. It looked like a real
backyard with grass and everything. A white
fence wrapped around to the back side of the
tan house with a red door. Of course the house
wasn't a real house. It was just a single wall
built and painted to look like one.

The girls frowned when they spotted Jack standing near the set. They quickly ducked under the snack table unnoticed. They watched Mom sit down on the ground to talk to the dog. The black husky puppy looked at her with his big blue eyes. He tilted his head to the side and stared at her. She spoke to him like he was a person.

"When you walk up and see the bowl of dog treats, I want you to pause and look into the camera. Then since you can't actually talk, smile big as if you're saying, 'Yum!' I want those dog treats so bad I'd do anything to get one."

Mom addressed the pretty actress on set, "I want you to be standing here next to the fence. Grab a bacon treat out of the bowl, then smile down at the dog."

The actress listened to Mom and nodded. Mom got down and spoke to the dog again. "Don't rush it. Look up at her. Smile big. Then do your special trick. Two back flips in a row. Got it?"

Taco barked... except the girls now knew for sure that he was Bingo. His tongue rolled out of his mouth as he did his famous smile.

"Perfect! Glad to see I'm working with a professional," Mom said as she stood and tossed the dog a treat.

"Don't worry," Jack responded. "I promise he will do the trick just like you want. Can you tell me when I'm gonna get paid for this?"

"We always pay cast and crew at the end of the day," Mom explained.

Giselle's phone buzzed in her pocket. The text message from Austen read:

I'M ON MY WAY.

"Austen's coming! What's the plan Evangeline?" said Giselle.

"To get Bingo back," she answered. Evangeline sneakily reached up onto the snack table. She felt around until she found the cheese balls and grabbed a handful.

Giselle glared at her sister as she popped the cheese balls into her mouth one by one. "You said you had a plan!"

"I do. My plan is to get Bingo back," said Evangeline with her mouth full of food.

"How? That's NOT a plan," Giselle responded angrily. She was totally going to look like a fool in front of Austen.

"Oh. Okay," Evangeline said, grabbing more cheese balls. "Then I guess I'm working on a new plan."

"I've got it! Let's just steal the dog back,"

said Mercedes.

Giselle grew more impatient by the second, "And when our parents don't have a dog for their commercial... then what?"

"I can star in it. Obviously!" Mercedes said.

"Without a dog they will get fired," explained Giselle. "It's a commercial for dog treats!"

Once again Giselle felt it was up to her to fix everything. She had to do it fast before Austen arrived. She looked over to the set and saw Dad talking to himself. He often did this when he was trying to solve a problem.

Dad looked closely at the dog collar camera. "Why isn't this working? Everything was perfect when I tested it. Maybe a new battery?" Dad tried to open the battery door, but it was stuck. He used a small screwdriver to carefully force open the tiny door. That's when he saw it... a fruit snack! "Evangeline!" he groaned.

Giselle frowned at Evangeline, "I asked you to put the collar back."

"I did. But you didn't ask me to put the battery back so I left that under the fridge," she replied.

Dad thought he was the most annoyed person on set until he looked over and saw Simon, the owner of Organic Bacon Treats. He was a very tall thin man and he wore an ugly brown suit that made him look like a piece of bacon.

Mom saw Simon too and knew they'd better get started if they wanted to keep their client happy. She ran over to Dad and whispered, "How much longer?"

"Just two shakes of a dog's tail," joked Dad as he showed Mom the fruit snack and the missing battery. Dad ran off to find another battery in his gear bag.

Mom groaned as she walked over to Simon. "I know we're running a little late, but it'll be worth it," she said to him.

"I hope so," said Simon. "This is already costing me more than I wanted to spend in the first place."

Mom tried to hide the fact she was stressed and smiled big, "It's going to be an amazing commercial. I can't wait for you to see what we have planned."

Just then Mom saw a member of her team pick up the hose on the backyard set. He turned on the water from the hose and filled up the dog's water bowl. "No no no!" she yelled as she ran over. "We need to use bottled water for the bowl. It's more clear and looks better on camera."

The man hurriedly took the bowl off set. Mom hung the hose back on the side of the fake house. She wanted everything to be perfect for the commercial.

"Got it!" yelled Dad. He put the new battery into the collar. "We're ready to roll."

"Okay people, this is not a practice. Everyone back to one," yelled Mom.

The sisters watched from under the table as the crew hurried around moving things on set.

"Oh no! They're starting," said Mercedes. "What are we going to do?"

Giselle quickly put her hand over Mercedes' mouth. Giselle used her eyes to point down to the ground. A pair of blue sneakers stood next to them. "It's Jack," she whispered.

The girls froze. If Jack saw them he might panic and take the dog before they could expose him. Jack scanned the table of treats and grabbed a handful of jelly beans from the bowl. The actress from the commercial walked past him.

"Hey! What are you doing?" she said, "They called actors to set, so get your dog."

Jack dumped the jelly beans back into the bowl and followed her. As he walked away the girls unfroze. Fewf!

Giselle's eyes darted around the studio trying to think of a plan. Her phone buzzed with another text from Austen saying he was almost there. "Oh no, oh no, oh no!" she whispered to herself. She felt a tap on her shoulder.

"Where's Evangeline?" asked Mercedes.

They looked everywhere, but Evangeline was gone. Uh oh. They couldn't believe she would have wandered off now when they needed her help.

"We're ready and rolling," yelled Dad.

"Action!" Mom shouted as she looked through the big film camera.

The commercial burst to life instantly. The leading actress smiled and spoke as she walked across the fake backyard. "Here boy!" she called out.

Bingo ran by the fence and up to the actress. Dad smiled as he watched the special collar camera video on his phone. The shot looked even better than he had hoped!

The actress continued her lines to the camera, "I give only the best treats to my dog made with organic ingredients." She turned to the dog and smiled. "Okay boy! Do you want a yummy organic bacon treat?

The actress held the bacon treat above Bingo's mouth. Mom was on the edge of her director's chair. She held her breath. Would the dog do the back flips like he was supposed to? Bingo's tail wagged. He started to jump.

All of a sudden another dog jumped in front of him and stole the bacon treat. It was Evangeline! But she kept her head down so her face wouldn't be seen. She barked loudly as she ran fast on her hands and knees. She barked and barked causing Bingo to get excited and chase her.

"Cut!" yelled Mom. "That was almost perfect! Why is someone in a dog costume on my set?"

"I'm calling security," said Dad as he dialed his phone.

Giselle and Mercedes were still watching from under the table. Evangeline got Bingo to bark loudly. They ran in circles around the fake yard.

"What is she doing? We're going to be in so much trouble," Giselle said worriedly.

Mom turned to Jack, "Can you calm down your dog? Please!"

Jack ran up to the set yelling, "Quiet! No!

Bad dog! No!"

Evangeline howled at Jack causing Bingo to growl. Bingo barked and snarled, which made Jack stand very still. This wasn't the first time Jack had dealt with an angry dog. He knew what to do.

Jack used a calm and quiet voice, "Nice dog. Now be a good dog and stop." He walked slowly toward Bingo and reached out his hands. Evangeline and Bingo kept growling and slowly backed up as Jack came closer.

Giselle's heart raced. A security officer was running toward the set. Any second they would grab Evangeline and they would all be busted. There was no way their parents would listen to their story about the stolen dog after that.

"Arf! Arf!" Evangeline barked panicking. She kept her head down so her face couldn't be seen.

Jack had forced them into a corner where the house connected to the fence. Evangeline and Bingo were trapped.

Giselle gasped, "I know what to do!" She jumped into action and ran as fast as she could toward the set.

Mercedes had no idea what Giselle was about to do, but she knew she should film it. She jumped up from behind the table and pointed her phone camera toward the set. "And action!" she said to herself.

Giselle was running so fast she could barely stop. SMACK! She hit the wall of the house. Quickly she grabbed the hose and turned the nozzle on full force. The stream of water went everywhere spraying Jack, Evangeline, and Bingo. Within a few seconds they were all soaked.

Mom recognized Giselle holding the hose, "Stop! No. Giselle stop!" she said as she ran toward her.

Dad got to the hose first and turned off the water. Everyone started yelling.

"Giselle, what are you doing?" shouted Dad.

"You gotta listen to me," she pleaded.

The security guard spoke louder than both of them, "Someone needs to tell me what is going on here. Who's in charge?"

"I am," said Mom.

Evangeline ran up to Mom dripping wet, "Mom, that dog isn't Taco!"

"Evangeline? You're the one in the dog costume?" Mom groaned. "You're supposed to be at home!"

Then Simon shouted at the top of his lungs, "QUIET! I demand to know what is going on."

The room grew silent. Giselle tried to speak, but she was so nervous all that came out of her mouth was a whisper, "Pup-napped."

Simon was even more confused, "What?"

Giselle cleared her throat. "Umm. Sir. The dog was pup-napped."

"That guy Jack stole him!" Evangeline said sure of herself. She pointed to where Jack had been standing, but he was gone.

Everyone was so busy arguing that no one saw Jack had grabbed Bingo and quietly snuck away.

Mercedes screamed at the top of her lungs. She pointed to Jack and yelled, "There's the scumbag!" She held the camera filming herself as she spoke. "Guys meet Jack. He's the bad guy we've been telling you about."

Jack turned back to the group on set. "You people are crazy. This is my dog Taco," he said. Jack held Bingo very close and still to his chest so the wet dog couldn't move.

Giselle addressed her parents, "Mom. Dad. That dog's name is Bingo and he belongs to a boy named Austen. Jack dyed the dog's fur black to make him look like a different dog. I can prove it."

"That's it. We're leaving," said Jack. "You

can find another dog for your commercial." He whipped around and started to walk away.

Giselle lost her cool and shouted at Jack, "You did it! You know you did!" She looked to her Mom for support. "You have to believe us."

Just then a bacon treat flew in the air by Jack's head. Evangeline yelled, "Bingo catch!"

In a flash, Bingo wiggled free and jumped from Jack's arms. He grabbed the treat in the air and landed with it in his mouth.

Everyone gasped. Jack's shirt and hands were covered in black dye. Bingo sat chewing on his dog treat. His wet fur dripped small puddles of black dye on the ground.

The security officer walked up to Jack holding handcuffs. "Let's try this again, but this time how about you tell the truth?" he said.

"If he tries to lie I've got the whole thing on video," Mercedes said smiling. She took a quick picture of herself giving a big thumbs up and Jack in the background in handcuffs.

"Case closed!" said Evangeline proudly. She popped open a victory can of dog treats. She tossed one high in the air and it landed in her mouth. Everyone on set stared as she chewed.

"Hey those aren't for kids," said Mom.

"Why not? They're organic," replied

Evangeline with a smile. Everyone laughed. She held out another treat for Bingo. "How bad do you want this?" she asked.

He jumped high in the air and then did his special trick. Two back flips in a row. Everyone cheered! Evangeline tossed Bingo the treat and then ate another one herself.

Mom didn't have time to lecture Evangeline right now. "I'll be back to talk about this," she said as she left to join Dad and Simon.

"We did it! I can't believe it," Giselle said as she did a dorky victory dance.

Evangeline held out another treat for Bingo. "Let's see that again!" she said as Bingo did two more back flips, this time even higher.

"Bingo!" yelled Austen as he ran up to the girls.

The sound of Austen's voice took Giselle by surprise. She stopped dancing and tried to play it cool.

Bingo jumped into Austen's arms. The dog licked his face, clearly happy to see him again.

"Hey bud! I missed you too!" he said giggling as the dog gave him more doggie kisses. "Where did you find him? And why is he all black and sticky?" he asked the girls.

"It's kind of a long story," said Mercedes.

"But we can tell you after we get paid."

Giselle elbowed Mercedes in the ribs and gave her a stern look. She smiled at Austen and said, "No need to pay us. We were glad to help."

Mercedes gasped in outrage, but before she could disagree, Evangeline spoke up. "Yup. No payment necessary. We're just happy we found him!"

Austen held Bingo tight as he looked into Giselle's eyes. "Well, maybe I can find another way to say thanks," he said smiling. He leaned in closer to her.

Giselle's heart raced. She couldn't believe it. Was she about to get her first kiss? LICK! LICK! Nope. Bingo beat Austen to it and happily licked Giselle all over her face.

Austen quickly pulled Bingo back. "Geez man! You gotta ask a pretty girl before you kiss her like that!"

They all laughed. Giselle blushed at Austen calling her pretty. It wasn't a kiss, but it was definitely a start to becoming Mrs. Austen... Hmm, she should probably figure out his last name before printing their wedding invites.

The girls were proud of themselves until they saw their parents talking to an unhappy looking Simon.

"I sure hope they don't get fired!" said Giselle. "We'd better go over there and explain."

The sisters listened to the conversation between Simon and their parents.

Simon sounded very serious as he spoke, "I've never been on a commercial set before. Is it always like this?"

Dad replied, "No. I can honestly say it's never, ever been like this."

Simon let out a big sigh. "Well, I don't know what else to say but..."

Giselle was about to interrupt when Simon's face lit up with a huge smile.

"I loved it! This little girl in the dog costume is hilarious!" he said pointing to Evangeline. "You two are full of surprises and what a fun new angle. The bacon treats taste so good, a kid tries to dress up like a dog and steal them! I say we go for it!"

Like always, Mom was quick on her feet to respond. Some people might say it's lying, but she and Mercedes called it acting. "I just knew you'd appreciate the creative process. Didn't I say that dear?"

Dad's mouth was still open in surprise. "Uh yes," he quickly responded.

Mom continued without missing a beat,

"I'm so glad you like it. With commercials, it's all about making something that people will talk about. That's why we wanted to show you how the commercial would look instead of just telling you."

"But I didn't quite get the part about the pup-napper and the security guard," said Simon confused. "Maybe we should cut that out."

Mom nodded yes, "I totally agree." Then she turned to the girls with a huge smile on her face. She quietly whispered through her teeth, "We will talk about this mess at home."

The girls looked at each other and smiled back. At least Mom would be in a good mood when they got in trouble.

Simon noticed Austen standing there holding Bingo. "And this guy!" he said as he rubbed Bingo's head. "Two back flips in a row, that's remarkable!"

Bingo barked and stuck out his paw. Simon grabbed Bingo's paw and shook it. He looked at the black dye that rubbed off on his hand, "But I think let's go without dying his fur black. The company believes natural is best."

"So you still want Bingo to be in the commercial?" asked Austen.

"Young man," said Simon in a serious voice, "I'm putting his face on the can! Your dog is going to be a star!"

CHAPTER 11

The whole family was at home gathered in the living room. A week had passed since the GEM Sisters had found Bingo. Excitement filled the room because any minute the commercial was going to be on TV. Dad passed out bowls of popcorn to everyone.

Evangeline popped open a new can of bacon dog treats, this time with Bingo's smiling face on the label. She sprinkled some on top of her popcorn.

Mom grabbed the can from Evangeline. "Okay you. Now that we're done with the commercial it's time to go back to eating human food."

"Not a problem," said Evangeline. She shoved a handful of dog treat popcorn into her mouth. "I know Bingo is addicted to these things, but not me. Totally got it under control."

Evangeline waited until her Mom turned away. She reached under the couch pillow and grabbed a hidden can of treats. Sneakily she sprinkled more bacon onto her popcorn.

Dad threw a piece of popcorn high in the air and Giselle caught it in her mouth. "Nice one!" he cheered. Dad threw one toward Mercedes who wasn't looking. The popcorn hit her on the cheek.

"Dad! Hey?" Mercedes said annoyed. "I just put on new lipgloss!"

Giselle's phone buzzed a new message alert. On the screen was a picture of Austen and Bingo happily sitting on the couch. "Aww how cute! Austen and Bingo are watching too," Giselle announced to the family.

She held out her arm and took a picture of the whole family smiling on the couch. She read aloud as she typed a message back, "Us too! We're so excited." As she hit the send button she accidentally pressed a heart emoji. Oh no!

In a panic, Giselle stared at the screen not knowing what to do. How could she send a heart emoji? What would Austen think? Her phone buzzed. Austen sent her a heart emoji back. Giselle's face lit up. She smiled and hugged her phone.

"We're really proud of you girls for helping Austen find his dog," said Dad.

Mom nodded in agreement. "Although I still don't understand how you knew that Jack had dyed Bingo's fur black."

"Seriously, like we told you, it was so obvious," said Mercedes. "We saw the flyer and then we saw the headshot picture. We solved it in like five minutes."

Mercedes knew Mom wasn't totally buying the girls' story. Fortunately the commercial started before Mom could ask more questions. The sisters had decided not to tell their parents everything that had happened. Why have them worry now that it was all over?

Dad shushed everyone. His eyes grew wide as he watched the opening shot of the commercial that was filmed with his new collar camera. "Look how great that fence looks with the dog's eye view!"

Next on screen they saw the pretty actress set a bowl of bacon treats on the ground. "For my family, I want only the best ingredients," she said. Bingo ran up and did two perfect back flips. The actress turned away and Bingo took a big slobbery bite.

Then Evangeline ran up in her dog costume

on her hands and knees. She stuck her head in the bowl and ate a treat too.

"Hey! Those aren't for kids," said the actress smiling.

Evangeline looked to the camera. She grinned and said, "Why not? They're organic!" then took another bite.

Everyone but Mercedes clapped and cheered as the commercial ended.

"This is so unfair!" whined Mercedes. "I wanted to be in the commercial. It should have been my big break!"

"Maybe next time you'll put on the dog costume when I ask," Giselle said with a smirk.

"Guess I'll be the most famous sister now," joked Evangeline to Mercedes.

Mom's phone rang. She shushed everyone, then answered the call. Dad and the girls could only hear Mom's side of the conversation. A big smile grew on her face. She looked at Dad and gave him a thumbs up.

"Oh that definitely sounds like something we'd be interested in," said Mom. "Of course, we'd love to meet with you tomorrow. Yes, we will come with lots of fun ideas. Thank you. See you then." Mom hung up the phone and did a happy dance.

"That was a new client," she explained. "It's a clothing store and they want us to shoot a video for their new fashion line!"

"I call being in the video," shouted Mercedes as she raised her hand.

"Sorry Mercedes, it's for baby clothes," Mom answered.

"But Mercedes always acts like a baby. Doesn't that make her perfect?" joked Giselle.

"Okay get along you two," said Dad. "How about we help you girls film a new GEM Sisters video tomorrow after our meeting?"

"And Mercedes you can be the star," Mom agreed. "Come up with the idea, and we will help you film it."

"Hmm. Okay," Mercedes said with an evil grin, "I've got a few ideas that I'd love to force my sisters to do."

"I don't like that look on her face," worried Evangeline.

"We better brainstorm some ideas for our meeting tomorrow," said Dad.

"What about dinner?" asked Mom. "I can whip up a batch of cold spinach soup pretty fast."

Dad saw the worried look on his daughters' faces, "I'm pretty full from the popcorn," he quickly responded.

"Super full," said Giselle as she patted her tummy.

"I couldn't eat another bacon treat," groaned Evangeline.

Mom didn't push the issue because the new client had her mind racing. "Fine. I'll just make it tomorrow," she said skipping down the hall to her office.

Dad whispered to the girls as he left the room, "I'll order us a pizza later. A good pizza, not Mom pizza."

Mom yelled from down the hall, "Honey! Get in here! I just got two more calls from new clients! I need you to talk to this woman who runs a horse camp."

Giselle's phone buzzed another message from Austen. This time it was a picture of Bingo laying on his back making a silly face. She showed her sisters the picture and asked, "Do you guys really think Jack would have returned Bingo after the commercial?"

"Well, Jack did say he only needed Bingo for the money. Then he was going to pay off his van and give him back," Mercedes answered. "But I would have kept the dog. I mean, why clean gross dogs for a living when you could have a famous dog instead?"

"Trust me, once you start a life of crime it's hard to turn back," Evangeline said in a serious voice. She looked around the room for another hidden can of dog treats.

"I just can't believe that we actually found Bingo. And we proved Jack was the pup-napper," Giselle said proud of herself. "I know my A+ essay on spies totally helped us out."

"Umm. I'm the one who found most of the clues. And I filmed all those videos to show the police that Jack was guilty," added Mercedes.

"Listen you two. If it wasn't for me talking to Austen at the audition, we wouldn't have had a case in the first place," Evangeline stated as she looked under the couch.

Giselle agreed, "Well I guess working together, we're pretty good at this detective thing."

"We should do it again!" Evangeline said eagerly.

"No way. I am so glad it's all over. I need to get back to my acting career," Mercedes complained as she looked at her nails. "We are filming my video tomorrow and look at this manicure emergency."

"You can still make GEM Sisters' videos

and solve mysteries Mercedes," explained Evangeline. "And Giselle with your nerdy school stuff, you can teach us more detective things."

"For once I agree with Mercedes," said Giselle. "I said we were good at solving this case together. I didn't say we should do it again. Case closed."

"But we had so much fun," argued Evangeline.

Giselle laughed, "It was pretty funny watching Mercedes being chased by all those dogs."

"Fun! You call detective work fun?" asked Mercedes. "Fun is going shopping not digging through stinky dog trash."

"Well, it takes money to go shopping," said Evangeline. "We could get lots of it for solving cases."

"If you guys didn't give it back, we would already have $500," Mercedes glared.

"Think about it. We could help people," explained Evangeline. "Maybe there are kids at school who need our help. Or rich people with stolen jewelry. Or I don't know, really old neighbors who lost their remote. We could find hidden treasure, or we could solve mysteries no one else can, like maybe even find Bigfoot. And we can call ourselves the Sister Detectives. We'll be famous!"

"Wait. You really think we could be famous?" asked Mercedes.

Evangeline nodded her head yes, "Like magazine cover famous."

"I didn't think about all the people we could help," said Giselle. "And we are pretty good at solving mysteries together. You know what, I'm in!"

Mercedes thought about the idea for a moment. "Nope. You two can play detectives without me. Becoming a superstar takes every moment of my day."

"But, we can't be detectives without you," whined Evangeline. "We're the GEM Sisters."

"If it wasn't for you, we would have never solved the case," pleaded Giselle. "We work great as a team because we're all good at different things. And you are scary good at lying."

"Hmm. It would give me a chance to practice my acting skills," Mercedes thought out loud. "I could play all different kinds of characters."

"And you looked so fashionable when you were digging in the trash," added Evangeline trying to convince her.

"Think of all the social media pictures you could take solving cases," said Giselle.

"We need you," begged Evangeline.

Mercedes locked eyes with her sisters. "So what you're saying is... I'm the most important member of the team."

Evangeline and Giselle rolled their eyes at each other, but decided not to argue with her. They both forced a smile and nodded yes.

"I guess I could help out, since you clearly can't do it without me," taunted Mercedes. "But, next time we're keeping the reward money."

"And next time, I need both of you to listen to me and do what I say," said Giselle in a firm voice. "I am the oldest, so I'm in charge."

As soon as she said it, her sisters burst out laughing. They had never listened to her before so why did she think they would start now?

"Just promise me when we're on the case you'll stay out of trouble," begged Giselle.

"I never make promises I can't keep," Evangeline answered. "But I promise I'll try."

"Sister Detectives. That's a great name Evangeline," said Mercedes. "Sounds like a TV show or a movie."

"Ooh! Maybe we could be like the author who wrote about the great detective Sherlock Holmes. We can write down all of the mysteries we solve and put them in a book!" Giselle said excitedly.

"I like my movie idea better," responded Mercedes.

Giselle turned to Evangeline. "So how do we find our next case?"

"How should I know? I'm just a kid," she responded.

Giselle thought about it for a moment. "I guess we just keep our eyes open."

"Maybe our fans have a case that needs to be solved," Mercedes said as she grabbed her phone and started filming. "Hey guys! So we have decided to start solving mysteries. We're calling ourselves Sister Detectives. If you have a case that needs solving, tell us in the comments."

Mercedes blew a kiss to end her video. Giselle stopped her before she hit the post button.

"Wait!" shouted Giselle. "We're just getting started as detectives. Let's not tell our fans until we know we're not going to make fools of ourselves."

"I was just trying to help," said Mercedes as she deleted the video on her phone.

Giselle's phone buzzed. She smiled big as she looked at the screen. "Austen wants to us to come over and film a video."

"For Bingo's channel with all of his fans? Tell him yes!" Mercedes said excitedly.

"Hey! You said Bingo's name the right way," realized Giselle.

"No, I didn't. I said BingBing. Please. I'm too important to remember a dog's name," said Mercedes. She quickly changed the subject, "I need to go touch up my hair."

Giselle looked at Evangeline. "Austen said to bring your dog costume."

"No!" Mercedes yelled. "This time I'm wearing it!" She ran out of the room to go put it on.

"Why does Austen want me to bring the dog costume?" asked Evangeline.

"He doesn't," Giselle responded. "I just want Mercedes to make a fool of herself in the video."

"Nice one," Evangeline responded proudly. "I like evil Giselle." Evangeline jumped up off the couch. "I need to pack some snacks for me and Bingo."

In a mad dash she pulled all the pillows

off the couch. She lifted up the cushions then looked behind the curtains and above the bookshelf.

"What are you doing?" asked Giselle.

"Looking for bacon treats. I used my last can on the popcorn," said Evangeline sadly. She reached her hand under the rug. "Arf! Arf!" she barked excitedly. She pulled out one little bacon treat from under the rug. It was covered in dust and had a dead fly on top.

Giselle made a grossed out face as she watched Evangeline shake off the fly. Evangeline opened her mouth and stuck out her tongue. She was about to take a bite but then slowly stopped.

She looked at the treat and then to Giselle. "Mom might be right. I think I'm addicted."

Mercedes entered the room wearing the dog costume. Both sisters couldn't help but laugh at how unhappy she looked.

"The things I have to do to become famous," she said with a sigh. Mercedes noticed Evangeline holding a bacon dog treat. "That's mine!" she shouted. "If you can be a dog actor then so can I."

She grabbed the bacon treat out of Evangeline's hand and shoved it in her mouth.

Giselle and Evangeline made gagging noises as they tried to hide their grossed out faces.

Mercedes chewed and chewed then finally swallowed. "Ew. Why do you like these? They taste terrible."

"Should we tell her about the fly?" Giselle asked Evangeline.

"Wait, what fly?" said Mercedes.

"No way," answered Evangeline.

"What fly?" yelled Mercedes.

"We'll tell you on the way to Austen's," said Giselle.

The girls giggled as they left the house. They couldn't wait to solve another mystery. The Sister Detectives had no idea that they were about to get their next big case.

Check Out The Next
Sister Detectives Mystery

The GEM Sisters can't wait to spend a whole fun week at camp together learning to ride horses. That is until they find out that the camp is haunted! Mercedes and Evangeline totally believe all of the camper's stories who swear they've seen the scary ghost horse running through camp. Giselle, on the other hand, doesn't think ghosts are real until she comes face to face with the ghost!

Now the Sister Detectives have to solve the mystery of the ghost horse before all of the campers leave and the camp is forced to close forever!

Support
Sister Detectives!

Leave An Amazon Review

Tell Your Friends About The Book

Share on Social Media

www.gemsisters.club

Meet GEM Sisters!
Join the GEM Sisters Club. It's free!
Get updates about a book signing near you!

About The Authors

MéLisa and Ryun have been partners in art and life for over 20 years. Together the authors share a passion for creating funny children and family entertainment for all ages to enjoy. When they're not penning books,  they're writing comedy sketches and funny videos with their daughters, the GEM Sisters, on their popular YouTube channel & website www.gemsisters.club.

Their inspiration for writing books came from encouraging their daughters to love reading as much as they did growing up. After an enthusiastic response from their first book, the authors have now penned multiple series with the wish that young readers everywhere will put down their small screens and open up their imagination. MéLisa and Ryun hope that their books will add a little laughter to your day. Current series include "Spy Pets" and "Sister Detectives."

MORE
Funny Mysteries
by The Authors

For Readers Ages 6-9
Buy On Amazon

Made in the USA
Middletown, DE
09 December 2020

26682918R00111